"I want a dance solo," Aimee Gillespie announced at lunch. "What about you, Maddie? What part do you wanna get?"

Madison Finn shrugged and took a sip of her chocolate milk.

The Far Hills Junior High administration had decided to organize a special cabaret in honor of the school's assistant principal, Mrs. B. Goode's, twenty years of distinguished service. They were planning three separate nights of entertainment—one for each class in the school. Everyone in the seventh grade was expected to try out for selected scenes and songs from *The Wiz*.

But Madison didn't want to. *She couldn't.*

Madison couldn't get up on stage to sing some lame rendition of "Happy Birthday" in the key of C.

She couldn't face having other classmates with their eyes fixed on her every onstage move.

And she absolutely couldn't dance.

Just the thought of auditioning made Madison woozier than woozy.

Even worse, Madison couldn't tell her friends that she didn't *want* to audition, especially her best friend, Aimee. Being afraid is one thing, but having to admit that to other people is another thing.

"Maybe I'll just be one of those creepy trees that talks," Madison finally told Aimee, trying to change the subject. "You know, like on the way to Oz."

"Yeah, Maddie, like that's the part you'd get." Aimee made a face.

"I'm serious," Madison said, flicking her straw at Aimee. Chocolate milk splattered across the orange lunch table.

"Don't get—ahh! My new top," Aimee cried. The milk just missed her.

She and Madison burst into a goofy fit of laughter.

"Morons," some kid with a buzz cut at the next table grunted. He looked like a ninth grader.

"Takes one to know one," Aimee muttered bravely under her breath.

Madison covered her face with her hands and turned back to the comfort of her lunch: two slices of bread, peanut butter, and a neatly peeled orange on the side. Orange was Madison's favorite color and her favorite fruit.

"Hello, superstars," Fiona Waters teased, sliding onto the lunch table bench alongside Aimee. Fiona was the new girl in town and at school, and Madison and Aimee were happy to have her as a new part of their group, along with their guy friends Walter "Egg" Diaz and his shadow, Drew Maxwell. Fiona's twin brother, Chet, usually hung out with them, too.

"Did you check out what Ivy's wearing today?" Fiona whispered.

The three girlfriends twisted their heads to catch a glimpse of Ivy Daly's showy blue-flowered dress.

"That's a Boop-Dee-Doop dress," Aimee sneered. "I saw it in a magazine this month. Figures *she'd* get it."

"She looks good, though, don't you think?" Fiona said.

"Whatever." Aimee's voice bristled.

Once upon a very long time ago, way back in third grade, Madison had been a best friend with Ivy, but things had changed a lot over the years. Now Ivy was known as *Poison* Ivy, enemy number one at Far Hills.

Aimee glanced over at the enemy again. "She'll probably get the lead in the play, just like always. She always gets what she wants."

"Uh-huh," Madison agreed, chewing an orange section.

Across the cafeteria, Ivy tossed her red curly hair and looked around the room. No matter how poisonous she acted, Madison thought, she always managed to get noticed. That was how she won the election for class president and how she won the attention of most boys in the seventh grade. She didn't have to worry about being liked by the popular crowd because Ivy Daly *was* the popular crowd.

"Let's talk about something else, please," Aimee pleaded. "Are you trying out for *The Wiz*, Fiona?"

"Will rehearsals conflict with soccer? I have team practice almost every day after school and—" Fiona paused. "Well, I can't miss soccer. I want to make a good impression with the coach, you know?"

Fiona and Madison had tried out together for the school soccer team, but only Fiona had actually made the team. Fiona had been a soccer star last year when she was living in California, so her making the Far Hills team was no big surprise. And Madison wasn't much of an athlete, so *not* making the team was no big surprise for her, either. Madison considered it a minor success, actually. She hadn't run away from team tryouts. That was something.

"Do you guys think I can do both at the same time?" Fiona asked.

"Totally," Aimee said. "We're only doing a few scenes, so we won't have rehearsals all the time. Mr. Gibbons schedules them in between normal after-school stuff—I think that's what I heard."

"I want to do both," Fiona said. "I love singing."

"Wait a minute. You play soccer, go to Spanish club, and you *sing*, too?" Madison said, a little surprised. She kept learning new things about her new friend. It seemed like Fiona was good at everything she tried to do—and she tried to do a lot. "When do you have time to do homework?"

"In between," Fiona said.

Madison stared down at the table, not saying much. She poured a molehill of sugar onto her lunch tray and traced a path with her fork. She didn't want Aimee to ask questions about the audition.

But it was too late. Aimee reached across the table for Madison's wrist.

"You still haven't said what you're gonna sing at auditions, Maddie!" Aimee cooed.

Before Madison could admit to being *all* nerves, Egg appeared out of nowhere. He stuck his head in between Aimee and Fiona.

"Are you guys talking about the show?" Egg said.

"Who wants to know?" Aimee growled back.

Egg swiped an apple off her tray and took a big bite. "After tomorrow's audition, everyone can call me *The Wizard*."

He put the apple back onto Aimee's tray.

"Wizard? You wish!" Aimee swatted at him. She glanced down at the bitten apple, dripping with his spit. "Soooo gross."

Drew, who was standing there, too, laughed. He stuck his hand up in the air and waved a silent hello to the rest of the table.

"Drew thinks I have a good shot at the part, so there," Egg said.

Fiona giggled. "You'll probably get the part, Walter," she said softly. "I mean, Egg." She bowed her head, and the beads on her braids clinked. Madison and Aimee both knew that Fiona had a giant, inexplicable crush on him.

Unfortunately Egg ignored her. Chet had walked up by now, and the three boys sat down in a cluster at the other end of the table.

"Whassup?" Chet mumbled.

"We're talking about auditions for *The Wiz*," Fiona said.

"Yeah," Madison jumped in. "Egg thinks he can be cast as—"

"A Munchkin," Aimee interrupted. "And I think that's a safe bet."

Chet cracked up. "Hey, fool! She got you."

Egg smirked. "And I'll get her back—when she least expects it."

"Well, I don't know what you guys are doing, but we're *all* trying out for the play tomorrow," Aimee said as she pointed to herself, Fiona, and Madison.

Madison leaned across the table, whispering, "Aimee, I'm not sure that I want to—"

The bell rang for the next period. In an instant

the group dumped their trays, grabbed their books, and exited the cafeteria doors.

"Ex-cuse me," Ivy said to Madison as she pushed her way to the door. "Watch it."

Ivy's annoying drones, Rose Thorn and Phony Joanie, followed close behind, pushing past Madison, too. They always traveled in a pack.

A rat pack, Madison thought as they scampered away.

Later that night, Madison asked her mom what she should do about *The Wiz*. She hoped Mom had the instant cure for all this audition anxiety, the way she poured eucalyptus oil in the bathtub when Madison had a cold.

"Gee, honey bear," Mom said gently, tickling her daughter's back. "No one says you have to audition."

"I have to be a part of the show, Mom." Madison sighed. "I can't just sit back and be scenery. I'm in junior high now."

"It could be a lot of fun. . . ."

"What's so *fun* about standing onstage while everyone and their parents stare at me?"

"William Shakespeare says, 'The play's the thing,'" Mom said. She paused. "You know who William Shakespeare is, right?"

"No duh, Mom. We read *Romeo and Juliet*, remember?"

"Rowrooooo!" Madison's dog, Phin, agreed.

The pug rushed over toward them, tail wagging in excited circles. His whole butt jerked as he huffed and puffed.

"Good doggy," Madison said as she bent down. Phinnie licked her chin. "What do *you* think I should do?" she asked him sweetly.

Mom came up with another suggestion. "If you don't want to act or sing, then why not try something else to help the show? You don't want to be a part of the scenery, but you could *paint* the scenery, right? You could paint a castle or something. Is there a castle in *The Wiz*?"

"I think." Madison shrugged.

"Well," Mom reached out to hug her daughter. "I know whatever you decide to do, it'll be great."

Before bed that night, Madison and Phin curled up in bed with her laptop computer. She punched in her secret password and opened a brand-new file.

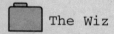 The Wiz

Rude Awakening: The play is definitely *not* the thing. I don't care what William Shakespeare says.

Or what Mom says.

Tomorrow they're holding auditions and tomorrow I am doomed. And of course Aimee won't understand when I tell her I can't try out. She'll say I'm just being chicken. It's so easy for her. And Fiona too.

Who knew that she could play soccer, look great, *and* sing? Well, she can. No one will understand why I'm so scared to try.

I remember one time when I had to sing Christmas carols onstage at school and I passed out, fell right there on the floor like a lump. Some teacher in a Santa suit had to carry me out of the assembly and everyone was staring.

What if that happens again? What if I faint or worse—throw up in front of the world?

What if *Hart Jones* sees me do that?

The whole time Hart followed me around in second grade he was SUCH a pest. Now why do I feel like following him? I saw him today in the hall when we left science class. I pray he didn't notice me staring.

If he tries out, I really think I should try out.

Madison decided her online keypal might know what to do. She hit SAVE and logged on to bigfishbowl.com, her favorite Internet site, looking for Bigwheels.

Usually Madison was suspicious of people she met inside the fishbowl since they sometimes made up facts about themselves. The Web site rules said you had to be "100% honest" about your facts, especially age and sex, but some kids weren't so honest. One time there was a boy in a chat room who pretended he was a girl. The moderator kicked him off for using dirty words.

Bigwheels was way different. Madison had met her over the summer in a room called ONLY THE LONELY. They now met back regularly in their own private room, GOFISHY. Bigwheels liked computers just like Madison. She gave great advice, too, which had come in handy since seventh grade started. They were kindred spirits in the virtual world.

Madison could share things with her online friend that she couldn't tell her other friends, not even Aimee or Fiona. Like her files, Madison still kept most things secret from the rest of the world.

Her crush on Hart Jones was one.

Bigwheels was another.

When she didn't find her keypal online, Madison wrote an e-mail to touch base.

```
From: MadFinn
To: Bigwheels
Subject: HELP
Date: Wed 27 Sept 9:46 PM
Thanks for your message from the
weekend. I wanted to write back
sooner, but I had like three hours
of homework. And now there's this
school play. Yikes. My friends don't
understand, but I don't want to
```

audition. I need your AMAZING
advice.

Yours till the curtain calls,
Madfinn

Madison hoped a megadose of "amazing" from Bigwheels would help her to make it through tomorrow's auditions.

Chapter 2

"Your alarm went off twice," Mom shouted. She tugged Madison's quilted comforter off the bed. "Now, up!"

Madison rolled into a ball. She *had* hit the snooze button on her combination CD-stereo-clock twice. Mom was right about that.

She would be late.

Madison pushed herself down, down, down into her mattress and pillows, where it was warm and safe from things like tests and teachers . . .

And auditions.

Phinnie licked Madison's nose as Mom appeared at the bedroom doorway again. "I am not going to ask you again, honey. I said get—"

"Up, up, I'm up," Madison groaned, finally lifting

herself into a sitting position. She pushed Phinnie out of the way and rubbed her eyes.

"Fifteen minutes and I want you ready to go." Mom dragged Phin out by the collar and shut the door behind her. "I'll get your breakfast ready."

"What would Aimee wear to an audition?" Madison asked herself a moment later as she posed in front of her closet. She sighed, pulling sweaters off the top shelf and throwing jeans, then corduroys and a long skirt into a pile on the floor. She finally decided on khakis, a white oxford shirt that she left untucked, and her favorite pair of orange sneakers. MADFINN was doodled in ballpoint pen on the left sole.

Madison stared at her reflection in her dresser mirror. Postcards and photos and ticket stubs wedged under the edge of its frame stared back. There was Aimee in jazz shoes; Phinnie at the beach; a close-up of a Brazilian frog from last summer's trip; Mom's business card for Budge Films; a receipt from Byte City, a nearby computer store; a pink ribbon from Lodge 12 at Camp Chipachu, where she'd won "Most Creative Camper" the summer after fourth grade; other pictures of Dad, Mom, and her newest pal, Fiona . . .

"Ten minutes and counting!" Mom screamed again. "I mean it!"

Phinnie was scratch-scratch-scratching at the door.

On her way out, Madison tripped over a pile of

files on the floor and then bent down to gather the colorful clippings that had slipped out. She'd been collecting files on all sorts of subjects for the last year: animals (she loved animals more than anything), cool words, clothes she wanted, singers she loved, flowers, and more. Madison had hopes of scanning all the words and images onto her computer and then onto her very own Web page.

What a mess, Madison thought. The more she tried to pick up the clippings, the more they went flying.

"Five minutes!" Mom screeched.

It felt like the beginning of the *worst* possible day.

When it was time for the afternoon seventh-grade auditions for *The Wiz*, Madison felt even more nervous than ever. In a study period, she went up to the library media center computer to check her e-mail, just in case Bigwheels had sent a message. But her mailbox was empty.

Nothing worse than an empty mailbox, Madison thought.

On top of everything else, she hadn't really seen much of Aimee or Fiona during the day. Everyone was way too busy thinking about *The Wiz* auditions to talk about other subjects. Tryouts had a wacky way of sucking everyone into the acting twilight zone so that suddenly even the quietest kids in school got stars in their eyes.

At the end of the day, as Madison entered the half darkness of the school auditorium, she felt a bolt of panic surge through her body like electricity. She zapped into a middle row of seats where Egg and Drew were sitting and sank down so no one could see her. It was almost like sinking under the bedroom covers this morning at home. Under those covers had to be the safest place on earth. Why wasn't she back there instead of in here?

"Has everyone filled out one of these?" Mr. Gibbons, Madison's English teacher and the drama advisor, waved a light blue piece of paper in front of the kids. "I want you to indicate what parts you want to play and what songs you'd like to sing. Put down your name and homeroom, too. Okay?"

Fiona came up from the seat behind Madison and whispered, "Did you see Hart Jones, Maddie? He told me he was looking for you. Oh yeah, do you have a pencil I can borrow?"

Hart?

Madison sunk deeper into her seat. The last person she felt like seeing right now was Hart Jones. She was in the middle of an audition freak-out. What possible reason could he have for wanting to see her *now*?

Mr. Gibbons dimmed the house lights as kids took the stage. It was hard to see anyone unless they were down in front or right next to you. A few people were even surrounded by a dim, red halo of light from exit signs at either side of the stage. Madison's eyes scanned the room.

Where were Ivy and her drones–Phony Joanie and Rose Thorn? *Down in front, right side of the room, talking to Mrs. Montefiore, the musical director.*

Aimee? *Down in front, mingling with another girl in Dance Troupe.*

Hart?

"Finnster!" Hart cried out of nowhere, and plopped into the seat right next to hers. He had been calling Madison that stupid nickname for years. He'd also been sitting behind her the whole time.

"Hello," Madison said. She was so surprised, she swallowed a great big gulp of air.

"Is this seat taken?" Hart joked, but of course he'd already made himself comfortable, leaning back and perching his sneakers on the row in front. "Hey, I wanted to ask you a question about the science homework."

"Ummm," Madison started to speak. Suddenly, without warning, she was out of the seat, pushing past Hart's legs, dashing up the aisle, heading out of the auditorium, running away.

Thunk.

The assembly doors banged open. Madison squinted. The light was brighter in the hall. The air was different, too. She leaned up against a giant trophy case and took a deep breath.

Inside the case were trophies for everything from

football to public speaking. Madison looked inside at all the names. This school was so much bigger than middle school; sometimes it felt overwhelming. Inside there was also a small display of autumn leaf art from the nature club and a bulletin board where the honor roll would be listed after the first marking period.

"Madison?"

She jumped and saw a boy standing near the water fountain.

"Drew!" Madison said, amazed. "You scared me. What are you doing out here?" Her voice echoed off the tiled walls and floors.

"You look wicked pale. Are you okay?"

Madison leaned past him to take a drink of cool water. "I'm okay. Just jumpy. Nervous about . . . you know . . . the audition."

"Me too."

"You are?" Madison asked.

"Yeah." Drew was looking at the floor.

"So what song are you gonna sing?"

"Oh no. I'm not auditioning," Drew said. "No way. I'm gonna work backstage instead. You know, lights, sound, that kind of stuff."

"Really? How did you learn about all that?" Madison asked.

"My older brother, Ben, did that in high school," Drew said.

"You have an older brother?" Madison was

intrigued. She didn't know too much about Drew's family except that he was super rich.

"Ben's from my dad's first marriage," Drew said. "He's in college now. We're not close, really."

"Oh," Madison said. Something in Drew's voice said to stop asking questions.

"Why don't you work backstage, too?" Drew suggested. "Why don't you ask Mr. Gibbons?"

Maybe Madison could work on the play *and* still be part of the group?

She smiled. "You think?"

"Yeah. Well. I gotta go." Drew shoved his hands inside his pockets and walked back inside the auditorium.

Madison followed. She could barely see her way down the aisle the moment the darkness enveloped her again. The only light now was a yellowish beam onstage, where one girl sat singing on a stool, holding a single high note. She sounded like an angel. Madison took a seat and watched until the girl had finished her song.

She was Lindsay Frost, and she'd been in Madison's class since first grade, but Madison rarely noticed her. The only time Lindsay spoke out in class was to ask for a bathroom pass.

Right now, however, Lindsay *and* her voice were making quite an impression on everyone.

"Thank you, Miss Frost," Mr. Gibbons said when Lindsay had finished her song. "I think I can speak for everyone when I say that was delightful."

"Even if she *can* sing, she's still a freak," someone whispered in the row directly ahead. Madison knew the voice. *Ivy Daly.*

"I can't believe she crawled out of her hole to try out," Rose Thorn whispered back. "As if she thinks she'll get in."

"As if," Phony Joanie said.

"*Fat* chance, right?" Ivy laughed at her own stupid joke. She always made cracks about the way people looked. It was one of the things that put her on the top of Madison's enemy list.

Before Madison knew what she was doing, she leaned forward. "Why don't you guys just shut up?"

Ivy whirled around. "Why don't you make me?"

"Shhhhhhhhhh!" Mr. Gibbons shushed them from down in front. "Keep it down, ladies, or you're out of here."

"Yeah, keep it down, Madison," Ivy said so everyone else heard. Rose and Joanie laughed.

Madison clenched her fists. She wanted to grab Ivy's pretty red hair and yank it out handful by curly handful until Ivy Daly was as bald as a big old bowling ball.

But Madison kept her cool.

She had something very important to discuss with Mr. Gibbons.

After Lindsay's song, a few other kids got up

onstage and tried to outdo one another. One kid even got up there and juggled while he sang.

Madison could feel the pound of a pulse behind her knees and on her wrists. It pounded more with each audition—the idea of her getting up there. It was like someone had turned her treble dial all the way up to the highest setting.

By the time she approached Mr. Gibbons, Madison was afraid she might not even be able to speak. Her mouth was dry, too.

"Not everyone is cut out for singing," Mr. Gibbons told her when they spoke. "I think I know what would be just perfect for you, though. . . ."

Madison's body hummed when he told her what she'd be doing.

She was bursting to tell someone her good news.

```
From: MadFinn
To: Bigwheels
Subject: Something Important to Tell
You
Date: Thurs 28 Sept 5:31 PM
```
Me again. Where are you? I know you are probably just busy again or your server is down again. But I still wish you would write! I was hoping that you would pick up the e-mail I sent yesterday and write back. Did you get it? Are you ok?

Didn't you tell me once you hated
acting? You didn't like people
pretending and being fake. Well,
after today, I *totally* agree.
What do you think about stage
managers?

THAT'S ME!

I just walked up to the advisor and
told him I was too nervous to go
onstage, and he said there was
other stuff for me to do. I have
to collect a few props and help
with line readings in case people
forget and organize their
costumes.

It should be a blast, don't ya
think?

Please write. I'm waiting!
Yours till the stage manages,

MadFinn

As Madison was signing off on her e-mail, an
Insta-Message popped up.

It was Fiona, a.k.a. Wetwinz. The pair ducked
into a private room to chat.

<Wetwinz>: I didn' t c u at the end of Wiz, what happened????

<MadFinn>: I didn' t try out

<Wetwinz>: what??

<MadFinn>: I didn' t try out

<Wetwinz>: WHY?

<MadFinn>: im gonna be stage manager instead

<Wetwinz>: oh

<MadFinn>: I told aimee all this on the phone didn' t she tell you

<Wetwinz>: Why?

<MadFinn>: I really wanted to do that. How was ur audition?

<Wetwinz>: I WUZ SO NERVOUS!!!!!!!!

<MadFinn>: Egg said you have a reallygood voice

<Wetwinz>: Egg did? What a QT! What else did he say

<MadFinn>: tell me how ur audition was

<Wetwinz>: no tell me more about Egg :>)

<MadFinn>: what about Ivy?

<Wetwinz>: she' ll get a good part

<MadFinn>: probably

<Wetwinz>: her voice cracked during that one song though

<MadFinn>: what else?

<Wetwinz>: time 4 dinner

<MadFinn>: DON' T BE NERVOUS L8R

Madison realized how happy she was *not* to be in Fiona's shoes right now.

She was happy not to be nervous anymore.

Madison had started the school day feeling like such a mess, but she was a long way away from "mess" now. She felt the same kind of calm that comes when a rainbow appears after a storm.

After the computer hummed and shut down, Madison crawled right back into the safest place in the world, under her quilted blankets. Phinnie crawled in beside her. Madison could feel his wet nose on her arm.

Soon she'd be asleep, and she'd be that much closer to tomorrow.

Closer to her debut as stage manager of *The Wiz*.

Chapter 3

"Don't push me!" Aimee shrieked when some kid with a backpack nearly mowed her over. They were standing in the hallway before seventh-grade lunch.

"Sorry," the kid said, pushing his way through anyhow. "You're the one in the way."

A very large crowd was trying to see the bulletin board on the second floor by the faculty elevator. There, on a piece of Mr. Gibbons's light blue paper, was posted the official cast of "Selections from *The Wiz*."

"Don't be nervous," Madison reminded Fiona as she locked arms with her. They gently nudged their way to the front.

Madison tugged Fiona's hand. "I can't believe it—look!"

"I can't believe it, either." Ivy groaned as she read the list. Her drones groaned, too.

Fiona just giggled.

CAST

Auntie Em	Roseanne Snyder
Toto	Chocolate (Mr. Gibbons's dog)
Dorothy	Lindsay Frost
Uncle Henry/Gatekeeper	Suresh Dhir
Evillene the Wicked Witch	Fiona Waters
Addaperle the Good Witch	Aimee Gillespie
Scarecrow	Thomas Kwong
Tin Man	Walter Diaz
Lion	Dan Ginsburg
Glinda the Good Witch	Ivy Daly
The Wiz	Hart Jones
Munchkins and Winkies	Zoe Bell, Beth Dunfey, Douglas Eklund, Lance Gregson, Joan Kenyon, Rashida Lawrence, Chet Waters, Tim Weinstein

CREW

Lights and Sound	Wayne Walsh and Class 9 Tech Club
Tech Assistants	Andrew Maxwell, Joey O'Neill
Choreography Assistant	Aimee Gillespie
Dance and Music	Mrs. Montefiore
Piano	Mr. Montefiore
Sets and Scenes	Mariah Diaz and Class 9 Art Club
Stage Manager	Madison Finn
Faculty Advisor	Mr. Gibbons

Ivy looked at the list. "Well, I didn't get Dorothy, but at least I got a big part. Glinda's a big part, right?"

Poison Ivy got the goody-goody princess role, Madison thought. It figured.

"I have to go talk to Mrs. Montefiore right away," Ivy said. She flipped her hair and walked away.

Fiona was *still* giggling. She'd gotten a good part, too. Better than she'd expected. "I like the way Evillene sounds."

Aimee waltzed over. "Oh my God, this is amazing—you got a lead! You totally rock, Fiona! And I get Addaperle! And a dance solo! And choreography assistant! I am sooooo psyched."

Fiona looked a little embarrassed by the attention, but she couldn't stop herself from beaming. Madison thought she looked more like a model than ever at that moment.

Egg, Drew, Chet, Hart, and even Tommy Kwong, king of drama club, bellied up to the bulletin board next. Madison watched them searching for their names on the blue list. Chet picked at his ear nervously. Egg bounced up and down like a jack-in-the-box. Drew, of course, played it quieter than quiet because he already knew what he was doing, just like Madison.

"Hey," Drew whispered, catching Madison's eye. "Congrats."

Madison grinned. "Yeah."

Drew slunk over to Egg, and the two of them pretended to bow down to Hart Jones. He'd been cast as none other than The Wiz himself, so he deserved the royal treatment.

Across the hall, Tommy Kwong celebrated his part with just as much fanfare. He was already practicing floppy-armed scarecrow antics, to the amusement of a group of girls who'd gotten chorus parts. As they oohed and aahed, Madison shimmied closer to Aimee and Fiona.

"I can't believe Poison Ivy is Glinda the Good Witch!" Aimee said.

Fiona's smile was wider than ever. "And I'm the *evil* witch," she said dreamily. "It's all pretty kooky."

They all laughed, and Madison gave Fiona a giant hug, one of those hugs where you don't let go right away.

"I am so glad you came to Far Hills," Madison told her.

"Excuse me." A girl walked up to the trio of friends and tapped Fiona on the shoulder. "Congratulations. You were so good at auditions."

"Thank you for saying that," Fiona said gently. "I'm sorry, I don't know you. I'm new. I'm Fiona Waters."

Madison recognized her right away. She was Lindsay Frost—the girl on the stool with the angel voice. Lindsay introduced herself. She wore an over-sized black sweater and chunky barrettes shaped like hearts.

"You were great at auditions," Madison said. "Everyone was mesmerized." She glanced up at the list again. Lindsay had been cast as Dorothy.

"Gee, thanks," Lindsay said. "I've been taking singing lessons and singing in choir since I was in first grade. And I love L. Frank Baum's books more than anything."

"Frank who?" Aimee and Fiona asked at the same time.

"Duh, you guys know," Madison said. "The guy who wrote the real Oz books."

"Don't you know them? In *Ozma of Oz*, Dorothy helps to save a queen. It's great," Lindsay said. "And there's this character named Princess Langwidere who wears a different head each day. I can loan you my copies if you want."

"Oh," Aimee said, still not knowing what they were really talking about but pretending that she did. "Oh yeah. Those books."

"Oh yeah," Fiona added. "Those books are kooky."

Aimee snickered when Fiona used that word again.

"Well," Lindsay said. She tugged down on her sweater. It was all stretched out and baggy around her middle. "I have to go to my next class now.

You're in English with Ms. Quill, right, Aimee? Maybe I'll see you around."

"Maybe," Aimee said as she walked away.

"Thanks again, Lindsay!" Fiona called out. She turned back to Aimee and Madison. "She seems nice."

"For a geek," Aimee said.

"Aimee!" Madison yelled at her. "Sometimes you can be so harsh."

"Well, it's the truth, isn't it?" she defended herself. "Isn't it?"

"The truth is," Fiona chimed in, "you sound like Ivy when you say stuff like that."

Aimee looked a little hurt. She didn't want to be like Poison Ivy.

"How well do you know Lindsay, Maddie?" Fiona asked.

"Well, she's been in our grade forever," Madison said.

"But we're not *really* friends," Aimee clarified.

Fiona and Aimee wandered off to their next classes, but Madison went in a different direction. She thought about how someone who had seemed so invisible could suddenly steal the spotlight from Ivy Daly and her drones.

It was an interesting development.

That night was Madison's weekly dinner with Dad, a night she looked forward to all week long. Ever since

Mom and Dad had gotten the "Big D" last year, Madison had reserved Thursdays just for him— except for the one dinner when he brought his new girlfriend, Stephanie, along.

Tonight she couldn't wait to spill the beans about the show.

Dad picked Madison up a little bit late, as usual. Being late usually made Mom rant and rave about how inconsiderate he was, which Madison hated. Mom didn't seem to be bothered tonight.

"He's here! I'm going!" Madison cried out when she saw Dad pull into the driveway. Phinnie wailed, "Wawooooooo," as Madison closed the front door. He hated good-byes even more than Madison did.

"So," Dad said the moment Madison hopped into the front seat and buckled up. "Tell me all about the auditions for the play and don't leave anything out, not one detail."

As Madison explained, Dad shook his head and chuckled lightly to himself.

"What's so funny?" Madison asked.

"You're a chip off the old block, you know that?" Dad said. "When I was a kid, I remember getting so sick whenever I had to do anything in front of other people. I had a terrible case of stage fright. I couldn't even stand up in the classroom. All the kids would laugh at me. . . . It was bad news. Puke city."

"Puke? Gross, Dad. You? Really?"

"You bet. So I guess you can chalk this one up to

30

genes, Maddie. Blame your old dad for your case of nerves. Sorry, kid."

Madison reached over and touched his shoulder. "I don't mind, Dad. Not really. Besides, now I'm stage manager."

They arrived at Dad's downtown Far Hills loft just in time to see the last innings of a baseball game between the Mets and the Braves. Next to computers and collages, Madison loved baseball. She got *that* from her dad.

"Did you see that?" Dad yelled at the television set. "That was a strike! What? Is the ump blind?"

Madison was setting the dinner table for two while "Finn's Fantastic Meatballs" heated up in the oven. It was really just Swedish meatballs with noodles, but Dad named all his recipes. He even baked Madison Muffins once. They were supersweet.

"Hey, Dad, I forgot to ask—can you help me with my computer assignment tonight? I have a test coming up."

"Double play!" Dad yelled at the television. Then he turned to his daughter. "Did you say 'test,' Maddie? Didn't school just *start*?"

"Yeah, well. Time flies when you're in junior high. Will you help?"

Dad laughed and walked into the kitchen. "Of course I'll help." He kissed Madison's head. "I'm really proud of you, young lady. Have I told you that lately? You are a bright, smart . . ."

"Dad," Madison moaned. "Don't start. Please."

"Start what? Isn't it acceptable for a father to be proud of his little girl?"

"Yeah, but you get so sappy. You and Mom both do that. Anyway, sit down. Dinner's served." Madison set the serving dish on the dining room table. "Oh and for the record, Dad, I'm not a *little* girl."

Dad laughed. "I know that, honey," he said. "Believe me, I know."

When the baseball game ended in overtime, they finally logged on to Dad's computer. It was fancy, streamlined with a monitor edged in polished steel. Dad always had the highest-quality equipment. Plus he upgraded a lot.

"Let me quickly show you my new Web site," Dad said as he punched a few keys. When the computer turned on, a picture appeared.

Unfortunately it was Stephanie, Dad's new and annoying girlfriend.

"Oh," Madison said, staring at the screen. "It's her."

Just then, the screen dissolved into another picture. This one showed Madison and Phinnie. It was taken last year during a snowstorm.

"It's not just her. Look, Maddie." Dad punched a few more keys. "Most of my screen savers are photos of *you*."

Madison watched as the picture of her and Phin

in the snow dissolved into her school photo from last year, which then dissolved into a photo of Dad on water skis, and then into a photo of Madison waving from the inside of Dad's car.

The screen finally dissolved for the last time into wavy lines, and Dad's site booted up. A giant blue logo appeared with the words FINN FRONTIERS.

"That's my company," Dad said proudly. "Well, my newest venture." Dad had started and stopped a whole bunch of businesses in the past ten years. Mom called him a snake oil salesman sometimes, but Madison wasn't sure she knew what that meant, exactly.

"Wow, that's neat-o," Madison said. The logo rotated around and around, leaving a trail of blue "dust" on the screen.

Madison was prouder than proud that her dad was so "with it" where technology was concerned. She didn't know any other parents in her class into computers the way he was.

"Let's tackle your computer homework now," Dad said, exiting his company's screen. "I think we make a good team."

Madison agreed.

 Hart

Just got back from Dad's. I have a Swedish meatball stomachache. I also have Hart on the brain.

I talked to The Wiz a.k.a. Hart for a little while after science class. Every time I see him and talk to him alone now is like a big deal, I can't help it.

Can you say CUTE? Plus, he stopped me in the hall, not the other way around. What does that mean? I congratulated him and he congratulated me and how dumb is that? He will make THE BEST Wiz ever in the history of *The Wiz*.

I think Ivy likes him, too, which stinks. She always flirts and she will probably find a way to make herself the center of attention in *The Wiz and* get Hart, too. Aimee's right. She's not just playing a witch in the show. She is a real witch.

What would Bigwheels do right now? I bet she is popular with guys. I'm just guessing. Maybe she can help me with the play *and* with Hart.

That is, if she ever writes back.

Chapter 4

Madison thought about Bigwheels all weekend long. Something was obviously wrong. Her keypal had never taken this long to answer an e-mail.

But Sunday morning, when Madison checked her mailbox for like the twentieth time, it appeared.

From: Bigwheels
To: MadFinn
Subject: Re: Something Important to Tell You
Date: Sat 30 Sept 11:58 PM
It's late. Not like there's anyone for you to tell, but still don't tell anyone I was up this late, ok? I had trouble sleeping, so I went online. I'm really not allowed on the computer after ten.

My life is a little strange these
days in case you didn't notice.
Can't really describe why. Just is.
I haven't even been writing poems.
I haven't been writing you. I'll
tell you later. I have to go with
my grandfather tomorrow. Scratch
that. It *is* tomorrow. Whoops. I
have to go today, Sunday.

Sorry for being out of touch. I
hope your play is working out. I
think that guy you're crushing on
sounds nice.

Meet me Monday at GOFISHY, ok? I'll
be there around five. Don't forget.

Yours till the hot dogs,

Bigwheels

The e-mail from Bigwheels took Madison by BIG
surprise. She wasn't sure how to respond to
Bigwheels when *Bigwheels* needed advice. What do
you do when your secret online friend has a problem
and you can't tell anyone in the real world about it?

Madison wished she could ask Aimee, but Aimee
didn't even know Bigwheels existed! When Aimee
called that night, Madison decided to keep her
online secret and to talk about clothes instead.

"Have you decided what to wear to the first rehearsal?" Madison asked.

"Oh my God! Wearing? I don't know what I'm wearing! Am I supposed to wear something special?" Aimee sounded like she was in a panic. "What are *you* wearing?"

Madison sighed. "I asked you first, Aimee."

"I don't know. What are you wearing?"

Aimee talked in circles sometimes. It was like she was dancing even when she asked questions, bobbing back and forth.

"Why don't you just wear your flared pants," Madison finally said. "The blue ones."

"Maddie, those don't look good on me."

Even if Aimee couldn't figure out what to wear, she'd *always* have an opinion about what *not* to wear.

"Wear your gray sweater, then," Madison suggested.

"You're kidding, right?" Aimee scoffed.

The next morning, Madison was the one who had to laugh when she met Aimee on the way to school. Aimee had on the blue, flared pants with her gray sweater tied neatly around her neck. Madison had opted for a long black skirt, sneakers, and a purple cardigan sweater with little flowers across the top.

After classes ended, Madison was the first one into the auditorium for rehearsal that afternoon. She sat right down in front, waiting for Mr. Gibbons and all the other students who were picked as cast and crew to take their seats. The room seemed completely different today. It wasn't dark like before. The whole stage shone with bright white light that washed out the curtains and the floor, making it a warm and inviting place. Instead of nervousness, the room was brimming with excitement.

"Everyone settle down, please!" Mr. Gibbons said as he walked in. "I'm sorry to be late. But please don't use this as a reason for *you* to be late to rehearsals, okay?"

Madison turned around and raised her eyebrows in Egg's direction. He was late to everything.

"Now to begin our first meeting, I'd like to thank you all for being a part of this production," Mr. Gibbons continued. "As Will Shakespeare said, 'The play's the thing.'"

Madison smiled to herself.

"We're only doing a few numbers from *The Wiz*, so in all fairness the lines and songs have been divided up equally. I want all students to have an equal opportunity to really shine. I hope you—*no*—I *know* you will."

From the middle of the auditorium, a loud kid named Suresh stuck his fist in the air and yelled, "Yesss!" Everyone laughed.

"Okay, now, settle down." Mr. Gibbons chuckled. "We've got a lot of work ahead of us, and only a very short time to do it."

Mr. Gibbons explained that the seventh graders would be working with ninth graders in the school's tech club and art club to get things done. Madison was happier than happy to hear that. It meant working with Mariah Diaz, president of the art club and Egg's older sister. Aimee and Madison both felt that having Mariah around was like having an older sister of their own—and Egg didn't mind sharing.

Kids began flipping through the script pages. Madison could hear Ivy and Rose counting up how many lines they each had. Joanie was complaining that she hadn't gotten any kind of lead part.

Mr. Gibbons called everyone in the cast up to the stage to line up in a single row across, but it turned into an instant fiasco.

No one could get it straight. Kids were nudging and shoving all over the place. Finally Mr. Gibbons blew a whistle to get them to STOP! He wanted them in order by height. Simple? No. That took *another* five minutes to figure out.

Meanwhile the crew stayed seated out in the audience alone. The ninth-grade tech and art clubs had left the room, so the only backstage people remaining were Madison, Drew, and Joey O'Neill, a seventh-grade kid everyone called "Nose Plucker."

Sitting in the audience was like being on an island and looking over at the mainland. Madison started to get that sinking feeling again. But now she wasn't just sinking into pillows or seats or anywhere else.

She was just sinking.

Lindsay Frost was up on stage, slouching in her baggy jeans and T-shirt, her hair pulled back in the same barrettes she'd worn at auditions. She was standing right next to Poison Ivy, all decked out in low-slung pants and a short-sleeved sweater that had a kitty-cat decal on it. Madison saw the pair as the sun and moon of seventh grade, opposites traveling in the same sky.

When Mr. Gibbons asked them to pair up, Ivy left a two-foot space between herself and Lindsay. Ivy didn't want to be paired off with *her*.

Madison knew the real truth: Poison Ivy would much rather be in orbit with her own drone rather than someone she considered "uncool."

But none of it mattered in the end because Madison could see that Lindsay was oblivious to Ivy—and everyone else around her. She didn't seem to care about kitty decals or who was standing where.

Mr. Gibbons clapped as Mrs. Montefiore, the music teacher, played a few scales. She asked the now assembled line of kids to join.

"Vocal warm-ups, boys and girls!" she said. "Do, re, mi . . . That means you, too, Miss Daly. Come along now. Mr. Diaz, turn and face front NOW!"

40

Drew leaned over to Madison. "Aren't you glad you're down here and not up there?"

Madison nodded. "I guess."

But inside she felt differently.

Mr. Gibbons explained that on a stage, the place between the actors and the audience is called a fourth wall. It's what separates real life from the life of the play.

Right now, Madison felt like the wall was separating her from her friends.

When rehearsal ended, Madison felt much better. In a snap, her whole group was back together again by the lockers.

"Let's go hang at Freeze Palace," Egg said, looking at Aimee, Madison, Fiona, Chet, Drew, and Hart. "Come on, it's only four o'clock!"

"Cool," Hart said. "I gotta be home around five, though."

"Oh, Chet, we don't have to be home, do we?" Fiona asked her brother.

"I can't go, Egg. I have too much homework," Drew said.

Aimee suggested they go hang out at her dad's store, Book Web, instead of the ice cream place. The bookstore was closer to school.

"You could do homework, Drew," Aimee said. "My dad has three new computers in the cybercafé part of the store."

"Yeah?" Drew asked. "Are you going, Madison?"

"Yeah, Maddie, are you going?" Fiona asked, tugging on Madison's purple sweater.

Madison grabbed her orange bag. "Yeah. Let's go."

"Let's boogie." Aimee twirled around and pushed open the school doors.

Madison was gladder than glad about how things were working out.

Going to Book Web with the cast was a chance to break the fourth wall and be with her friends. Maybe she could even spend a little time with Hart?

Bigwheels would approve.

Chapter 5

"Hey, Daddy." Aimee kissed her father as they walked into his bookstore.

Aimee's oldest brother, Roger, was behind the Book Web counter, helping a man choose a book for his granddaughter. Roger was working there while he saved money for graduate school. He wanted to be a professor.

Other than that, the store wasn't too crowded.

"Is it okay if we hang out here for a little bit, Daddy?" Aimee asked.

Mr. Gillespie nodded and extended his hand. "Hello, Walter. And Andrew. And Maddie. And you're Fiona, right?" He introduced himself to Chet, too, and shuffled the group over to a large table near the back of the store. It was lodged between two giant bookshelves overflowing with used paperbacks.

After a chorus of awkward thank-yous, Mr. Gillespie disappeared into the back room.

Madison sat down first, then everyone else filtered over and squeezed in around her. The table really wasn't big enough for all seven of them, but they would make it fit. Madison couldn't believe it when Hart ended up squished on one side of her.

"Sorry," Hart said when his knee knocked hers.

Madison covered her cheeks because she was afraid she might be blushing.

"Okay, so what did you guys think of the first rehearsal?" Aimee asked the table. "I mean, I think Mr. Gibbons is so nice."

"Rose is a babe," Egg said.

Aimee slugged him. "Rose? Egg!"

"Finnster, what does Mr. Gibbons have you doing as stage manager?" Hart asked.

Madison could feel his breath, he was so close.

"Um, well . . ." Madison tried talking, but the words were lodged in her throat like grapes.

"That's great that your sister is helping with the set and costumes, Egg," Fiona piped up. "She's so glam."

"Glam?" Egg laughed so hard, he started to cough. "Don't make me laugh."

"She is, Egg!" Madison yelled. "Glamorous in her own way."

"This is boring. Let's go over to the computers," Chet said all of a sudden. Hart thought that was a great idea. As he jumped up to join the others, he kicked Madison, but she didn't mind.

Egg stood up. "We can go online from over there, too. Mr. Gillespie gave me the passwords."

Before the boys could move to the cyber part of the café, however, a woman rushed over and blocked their path.

"Well, hello," she said. "Aren't you all in my daughter's class?"

It was Mrs. Daly, Ivy's mother.

Everyone grinned back at her without saying a single word. Poison Ivy was right behind her.

"Ivy tells me your class is doing *The Wiz*," Mrs. Daly gushed. "That must be so much fun!"

No one said anything, but Mrs. Daly kept right on talking.

"I was in *The Wiz* in junior high, too—isn't that funny?" Mrs. Daly said. "Ivy, don't you want to say hello to your friends?"

"Hello," Ivy said curtly. She turned back to her mother. "Can we go now?"

"*The Wiz* is a great show, Mrs. Daly," Hart said. "I'm Hart Jones. I'm in *The Wiz* with Ivy."

"Oh really?" Mrs. Daly said, impressed.

"Hart's not in *The Wiz*, Mother," Ivy said, perking up for a moment. "He *is* The Wiz." She smiled right at Hart but avoided all eye contact with the three girls at the table.

"Actually, we're *all* in the play," Hart said,

gesturing to Madison, Aimee, Egg, Chet, Fiona, and Drew.

Everyone said hello. That's when Ivy's smile disappeared.

"Can we get your book and just go, Mother?" she said.

"Okay, dear." Mrs. Daly let out a deep sigh. "Good-bye and good luck to all of you. I can't wait to see it."

"Mother, let's GO." Ivy grabbed her mother's arm. Even though she was leaving, Ivy made a point of looking over her shoulder. She smiled at Hart one last time as she walked away.

Madison wanted to scream.

"Maybe we should have asked Ivy to stay and run lines with us?" Fiona whispered as Ivy and her mother walked away.

"What?" Aimee said. "I don't think so, Fiona. I mean, oh my God, she's usually so nasty to us, so why should we—"

"She's not nasty; she's cute," Chet said to Egg. All the boys laughed knowingly, even Hart. Ivy might be the meanest girl in class, but she also had the best hair and showed her perfect belly button whenever she had the chance. Boys loved that.

"Hey, check this out." Hart pointed to a page in his script. "In this scene I wear a big mask. And Fiona, you have to wear bad-witch makeup. Egg, are you gonna wear tinfoil as the Tin Man or what?"

Egg clapped him on the shoulder. "Ha, ha, ha, Hart."

Drew snorted.

Madison couldn't take her eyes off Hart. She wondered if she would be the one to help him put on his mask before the show.

She hoped.

Talking about all the costumes also made Madison think of her prop list. She went back through the script for items.

Crystal ball.

Lion's whiskers.

Special silver slippers.

Even with Mariah and the art club's help, Mr. Gibbons would have a lot of preparation to do—and Madison would be the one helping him do it. The role of stage manager now seemed way harder than just playing one part or singing one song.

"Wow, they're cutting a lot out of the original show." Hart flipped through the rest of his script pages. "'Selected scenes' means we lose half the songs."

Drew checked his watch for the tenth time. "Don't you guys have a test tomorrow? I do."

"Yeah, me too," Hart said. "I gotta fly."

"Is it five o'clock already?" Madison asked. She suddenly remembered her chat plans with Bigwheels. "I better get home to . . ."

She wasn't about to tell everyone there about

how she really had to hurry home to go in a special chat room to see what was wrong with her online friend's life.

". . . to walk Phinnie," Madison finished.

"Can't Phin use the dog door?" Aimee asked.

"Who's Phin?" Hart asked.

"Her pug," Fiona answered.

"The Finnster has a Phin?" Hart joked.

Egg mocked Hart. "Finnster has a Phin?" he said in a singsong voice.

"Hey, what about Blossom? She's a great doggy, too," Aimee boasted. She had a girl basset hound that loved to play with Phin. Madison and Aimee always joked if you put their two dogs together, they would make the ugliest, smushed-faced, floppy-eared pups.

"Are we staying or going . . . ?" Chet asked. "Or talking about *dogs*? Hello?"

Aimee shrugged. "*I'd* like to keep doing *The Wiz*. You guys have other places to be, obviously."

"People to see, places to go . . . " Egg cracked.

"Aimee," Fiona said, "*I* can stay a little longer if you want. We can still go over lines, just you and me."

Madison felt funny about leaving when she heard that. For some reason she didn't want to leave Aimee and Fiona alone. If she walked away, would Madison miss something important? She'd already missed the cast lineup and the singing rehearsal. She didn't want to miss anything else.

Egg was walking away. "Later, Aim." He nodded in Fiona's direction.

"Later, Egg." Fiona grinned right at him.

"Yo, Wicked Witch of the West." Chet waved his hand in front of his sister's face like he was waving her out of some kind of trance. "See you home."

"IM me, Maddie!" Fiona said, ignoring her brother.

"Call me later, 'kay?" Aimee called to Madison.

Madison waved to the pair. She was still reluctant to leave, but Bigwheels would be waiting.

The walk home went by slowly without Aimee and Fiona there to gossip. The streets were empty, the air was chilly, and the sun was beginning to sink in the western sky. Her bag weighed a ton and pulled heavily on her shoulder. She'd brought home her math textbook. She had the same test Hart did.

Since she was alone, Madison took a shortcut through the backyards of the houses just behind Blueberry Street, snagging her purple sweater as she tripped through a neighbor's garden and slid over a rock wall. It was still quite light out, but soon the sky would get darker and darker until all the pink disappeared.

With each stride, Madison secretly wished she were back at Book Web with Aimee and Fiona, even though she didn't have lines to memorize. Was being picked as stage manager less like being cast in the show and more like being cast *aside*?

"Stop over-thinking," Madison told herself.

Phin welcomed her home with a loud bark as soon as Madison walked in the door. She gave Phin a big hug, and the dog responded with a snort. Sometimes it was hard for pugs to breathe when they got overexcited.

Mom had left a note on the counter, explaining how she ducked out to do grocery shopping, so Madison grabbed a root beer and ran up to her room. The clock by her bed said almost half past five. She had to log on to bigfishbowl.com—fast. She went into the main fishbowl to find her keypal.

```
        SHARK (Moderator)
        MnMrox411
        TellMeAStORY
        Wohl_Consol
        ChuckD4Ever
        PrtyGrrl88
        12345Slim
        Brbiedoll


<TellMeAStORY>: get out
   MadFinn has entered the room.
<Wohl_Consol>: I mean it
<TellMeAStORY>: u lie
<PrtyGrrl88>: Hey MadFinn A/S/L?
```

Madison didn't like it when kids in the chat room waiting room asked for her A/S/L, which meant age, sex, and location. It made her uncomfortable, even with SHARK in the room. What if some creep-o was in the room, pretending to be some kid? Mom once told Madison some horror stories just so she'd stay safe.

The stories worked.

```
<PrtyGrrl88>: Finn . . . A/S/L?
<PrtyGrrl88>: Wohl . . . A/S/L?
<MnMrox411>: Who likes rap? Rap
   RULES
<PrtyGrrl88>: This room bites
<SHARK>: Watch your language
   PrtyGrrl88
PrtyGrrl88 has left the room.
Bigwheels has entered the room.
<Bigwheels>: MadFinn!
<MadFinn>: Let's go ASAP
<Bigwheels>: *poof*
```

Madison followed Bigwheels into GOFISHY. She was dying to hear what Bigwheels had to say.

```
<MadFinn>: HEY
<Bigwheels>: i missed u
<MadFinn>: me 2
<Bigwheels>: im sorry again bout the
   other day
<MadFinn>: no prob but whats
   wrong???
<Bigwheels>: %-(
```

<MadFinn>: wuzup? y r u sad?
<Bigwheels>: mom & dad
<MadFinn>: what happened?
<Bigwheels>: they're splitting up
<MadFinn>: IDGI
<Bigwheels>: it's a long story
<MadFinn>: can u tell me
<Bigwheels>: they told me they're
    separating
<MadFinn>: whoa
<Bigwheels>: I am in total shock
<MadFinn>: :-c
<Bigwheels>: my little sister
    doesn't even know
<MadFinn>: what did they tell u???
<Bigwheels>: they didn't say much
    just that they don't need time
    apart whatever that means
<MadFinn>: whoa
<Bigwheels>: your parents split up
    right?
<MadFinn>: yes
<Bigwheels>: how did u feel when
    they told u?
<MadFinn>: <rrr>
<Bigwheels>: it's so weird
<MadFinn>: I know
<Bigwheels>: what am I supposed to
    feel?
<MadFinn>: I'm sorry
<Bigwheels>: I'm just sad

52

```
<Bigwheels>: my mom is moving out
<MadFinn>: really?
<Bigwheels>: yeah usually the dad
    leaves right?
<MadFinn>: my dad did
<MadFinn>: hello?
<MadFinn>: Bigwheels?
<Bigwheels>: I have to go
<MadFinn>: can't you talk more? I
    want to know everything
<Bigwheels>: I have to go PAW and
```

Bigwheels signed off without even saying a real good-bye. Madison didn't know what to think.

She couldn't believe it.

Bigwheels's parents were splitting up just like Madison's parents had?

It was one of those moments when having an online friend didn't feel quite right. Madison couldn't reach out to give Bigwheels a hug. Her keypal was miles away.

But far away or not, Bigwheels was in trouble. The distance and the online separation didn't take away from that. Now Bigwheels needed Madison, not the other way around.

And Madison wanted to help.

Chapter 6

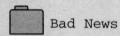 Bad News

I should have expected Tuesday would be
bad news before I even got to rehearsal.
Like when Bigwheels told me online last
night about her parents. I should have
known then. I figured seeing Fiona, Aimee,
and everyone else at rehearsal would fix
it. NOT.

Rude Awakening: It's hard to look at the
bright side of life when you're sitting in
the middle of a dark auditorium.

I couldn't stop thinking about Bigwheels
all day.

Thankfully, things got way better after
rehearsal ended. Aimee surprised me tonight
around six when she came over with a new CD
she bought. We danced around my room a

little. I am the worst dancer on the
planet, but that's ok. She got a letter
from one of her summer camp friends, too,
so we read it together while she French
braided my hair.

    I guess her glad erased my sad.
    I hope I stay this way.
    We have SUCH a busy week.

At Wednesday's rehearsal, Lindsay Frost walked into the auditorium and tripped over someone's backpack. She went flying into a row of seats and landed on her stomach.

She said she was fine, but Mr. Gibbons rushed her off to Nurse Shim.

It really *wasn't* a big deal. But after Lindsay left the auditorium, a few of the other cast members started buzzing about the whole thing. Ivy was plotting how she would become Dorothy once Lindsay had to drop out.

The Wiz seemed to be bringing out the worst in some of Madison's enemies *and* even her friends.

Lindsay came back a little while later with nothing more than a bump on her arm, an achy tummy, and a bruised ego. Mr. Gibbons was relieved.

So was Madison.

The idea of Ivy becoming the new Dorothy gave her the jeebies. The enemy would have more time to flirt with Hart if that were true.

"I am so embarrassed about tripping," Lindsay

confided in Madison during a break. "Was everyone laughing at me?"

Madison didn't know what to tell her. She shrugged. "I don't think so."

"I get so, so, SO nervous," Lindsay said. "The nurse told me I should go home and rest since my arm was hurt, but I didn't want to leave. This is too exciting, being in this show and all. Everyone is so nice."

"Yeah." Madison didn't know what to say.

Doesn't she get it? Everyone is NOT so nice.

Lindsay's arm looked like it had a dent in it. Madison kept nodding.

At the very end of rehearsal, Mr. Gibbons and Mrs. Montefiore asked Lindsay if she felt well enough to come onstage and practice "Ease on Down the Road," the song for Dorothy, the Scarecrow, the Tin Man, and the Lion.

There was a lot of commotion in the room, and no one was paying attention at first to the singers and dancers except for Madison. She might not have known what to *say* to Lindsay, but she knew she liked to *listen* to her.

Up on the stage, the cast in the other parts of the song goofed on Lindsay every time she moved. She did look a little off balance, but they were making way too big a production out of her being awkward.

Who cared how she moved? Lindsay *sounded* better than anyone in the auditorium.

"Look," Aimee said to Madison and Fiona. "I feel so bad for her. Does she know how *dumb* she looks?"

Fiona giggled. "It's her pants."

Being a mediocre dancer was no reason to be made a laughingstock, was it? Madison couldn't do a pirouette or a jazz turn, either.

"Her clothes are so lame," Aimee said. "And she's kinda klutzy. She should not be in a dance number. Definitely not."

Fiona nodded in agreement. "I see what you mean about the way she dresses. I wonder if that's why she's always alone. . . ."

"What are you guys talking about?" Madison asked. "She has a great voice. Why do you have to say stuff like—"

"It's not like we think she's a bad person or anything, Maddie," Aimee said. "She *can* sing, I admit it. It's just that she's different, right, Fiona?"

Madison knew what Aimee really meant. And it made her just a little sad.

The next afternoon, during Thursday's practice, Mr. Gibbons split the cast into smaller groups so characters could rehearse different scenes simultaneously. He sent the chorus members to the music room with Mr. Montefiore, other main characters stayed in the auditorium, and the crew stayed behind to tape the stage, label props, and do other backstage tasks.

Real-life cousins Hart and Drew joined members of the ninth-grade tech club to organize lighting and sound effects. They tested different-colored gels over the spotlights during Hart's solo "So You Wanted to Meet The Wizard." Green was the coolest-looking gel because when light shone through it, the green gel made the whole stage look like a rain forest. It reflected an eerie glow off Hart's face.

Madison thought he made a perfect wizard. *Perfect.*

One of Madison's key responsibilities for the day was to prompt lines for kids who forgot. Egg missed all his cues, but no one said anything. Even drama king Kwong spaced on a few bars of his song. Not one peep.

But when Lindsay forgot a few of her lines, *everyone* ribbed her. During the "Ease on Down the Road" number, Dan the Lion called her "Blimpie."

Madison was uncomfortable when she heard that, but Lindsay wasn't fazed. She didn't seem to care about anything people said behind her back or to her face. She sang her solo as beautifully as ever. Other people looked right through Lindsay like she was plastic wrap, but Madison was starting to see all of the things Lindsay had inside. She might be a different kind of friend, but something about her was special.

Mariah arrived in the auditorium at four o'clock.

She and Madison went into a room together back-stage to work with the home and careers teacher, Mrs. Perez. A group of kids was assembling some of the costumes.

"Excuse me." Mrs. Montefiore poked her head into the room where they were working. She needed to use the old practice piano in the corner so the three witches could run through their solo numbers.

Mrs. Perez moved her fabric, sequins, and other assorted garments into the corner. "Okay, we'll finish over *here*."

With everything that was going on in practice, it became difficult for Madison to focus on clothes. How can you help glue sequins on shirts when your best friend and worst enemy are singing scales ten feet away from you?

The only clothes Madison could seem to pay attention to were the ones on Ivy and Aimee. They were both wearing platform sneakers, canvas pants, and multicolored power bead bracelets. Aimee's blond ponytail perfectly matched Ivy's red one.

"Maddie!" Aimee called from the piano. "You're gonna love this. Listen up."

Madison waved over as if to say, "Yeah, sure, whatever."

"Maddie?" Aimee was raising her voice like she always did when she talked way too fast. "Didn't you hear what I—"

"Aimee, we ALL heard what you said," Ivy

quipped. "Uh . . . could you talk a little louder?" They were semi-snotty words, but she didn't say them in an obnoxious way. Ivy actually sounded like she was kidding around.

Ivy never kidded around like that.

"Oops! Bigmouth alert!" Aimee joked. "But is it me or . . . YOU?"

She made a funny face and Ivy laughed—one of those deep belly laughs. Their ponytails shook from side to side.

"Takes one to know one!" Ivy spit out, laughing.

Ivy never laughed like that.

Madison didn't see what was so funny.

"Now, remember how we did it last time, Addaperle. . . ." Ivy said.

"You bet, Glinda," Aimee said back.

Was this really happening? This trio should be sparring, not singing. And definitely not *smiling*.

Fiona leaned on the piano the whole time, laughing as hard and as long as Aimee and Ivy. Listening to their laughter was like coming down with chicken pox.

Please go away, Madison told herself. She itched all over.

"Tut, tut. Let's start, girls." Mrs. Montefiore hit a few piano keys.

Mariah also tapped Madison on the shoulder and reminded her they had a lot of work to do and not a lot of time to do it. She handed her a bag of big blue beads and asked Madison to string them on a long piece of cord. Madison sat down with her legs crossed and pulled the cord with both fingers. She could bead *and* keep her eye on the singing witches at the same time.

Mrs. Montefiore played Ivy's solo number from the end of the show next. But halfway through the introductory melody, she stopped abruptly.

"I just got a wonderful idea," she said. "Aimee, I want you and Ivy to sing this one as a duet. You're together in the scene. I think it makes sense. And your voices do sound lovely together."

"But it's my solo," Ivy barked.

Aimee rolled her eyes. "Solo, polo, rolo . . ."

They were kidding around again.

"Miss Daly," Mrs. Montefiore said. "Most solos have been turned into group numbers. This is about working together. To-geth-er."

"Can't Fiona sing, too?" Aimee asked.

Mrs. Montefiore shook her head. "Just do it the way I am asking, please. And Miss Waters is not in this scene, Miss Gillespie. She's the bad witch Evillene. At this point, she's dead."

Fiona giggled. "Oh yeah, I forgot."

Ivy tilted her head to one side like she had her head in an imaginary noose.

"Yeah." Fiona laughed even though it was a creepy gesture.

Mrs. Montefiore banged her fist on the side of

the piano for attention. She plinked out a few more piano chords that sounded a little out of tune, but Ivy and Aimee's voices trilled right along into the first stanza.

"'Believe what you fe-eeeee-el,'" they started to sing again. "'Because the time will come aroooooooound . . .'"

As they got louder, Madison had to admit that they *did* sound good together. Not as good as Lindsay, but better than Egg. By the second verse Aimee and Ivy were standing so close together at the piano, they looked practically attached.

"'Believe in the magic that's inside your heart,'" the pair harmonized. "'Believe what you seeeeee . . .'"

Madison couldn't believe what *she* was seeing at all.

"Pssst!" Mariah leaned down to speak. "Señorita Finn, how are those beads coming along?"

There were only seven blue beads on the cord. *Whoops.*

"Madison!" Mariah said. "Mrs. Perez is gonna throw a fit. What's your problem?"

Madison wanted to point at Ivy and Aimee and yell, "THEM!"

Instead she slid another bead onto the string.

For the rest of the day, Madison couldn't get the faces of Aimee and Ivy singing and smiling out of her head. And when Aimee didn't return Madison's phone call that night, it only made her feel worse.

Friday, Madison was feeling more of the same.

She didn't see Aimee all morning, which wasn't unusual since they didn't really have that many classes together, but her imagination started doing back flips.

What if Aimee was being nice to Ivy outside of rehearsal, too?

What if they were all laughing together right now?

What if they decided to become best friends and the joke was on Madison?

When Madison didn't see Aimee or Fiona at lunch, either, she got more upset. And although she ate with Egg and Drew that afternoon, Madison barely said a word the whole meal.

Mr. Gibbons took time to go over the master prop list with Madison during the day's rehearsal, and by then Madison was really bummed out. Luckily, his compliments temporarily put her in a better mood.

"What a great job you're doing," he praised. "*The Wiz* wouldn't be the same without you."

"Thanks, Mr. Gibbons," Madison replied sheepishly. She was pleased that at least her stage manager duties were working out. She wished doing good prop work would translate into an automatic A on all of Mr. Gibbons's English assignments. That would be something else.

"Gotcha!" Aimee shrieked as she came up behind Madison during the rehearsal break.

Madison nearly leaped out of her sneakers.

Aimee threw her arms around Madison's waist. "Where have you been?"

"Where have *you* been?" Madison asked.

"Me? You're the one who's so busy, you can't call me." Aimee poked at Madison's side. "I wanted to play you that song again from my new CD. It is so awesome, I can't stop listening to it."

"You called? When?" Madison asked.

"Last night. Before I walked the dog."

"But—"

"I left a message with your mom, but she said you were on the computer. I wanted to see if you wanted to walk Phinnie, too."

"You did?"

"Yeah!" Aimee was dancing around while she talked.

"I didn't get any message," Madison said.

"What? Did you think I blew you off or something?"

"No. Of course not." Madison paused.

"So what else is new?" Aimee asked, twirling around.

"I heard you doing that duet with Ivy yesterday."

"Oh yeah? What did you think? Pretty good, huh? Mrs. Montefiore is a big pain, but you know what? Ivy has a good voice, so it's actually working out," Aimee seemed pleased by the whole thing.

"Are we talking about the same Ivy? *Poison* Ivy?"

"Yeah, Poison Ivy. But she's really not so bad as far as the show goes. You know, when we're singing. She has a high voice. We were practicing today together during lunch."

"Oh?" Madison looked up at Aimee. "You had lunch with Ivy? Alone?"

"No," Aimee said. "Fiona was there."

"I wondered where you guys went."

Suddenly Aimee saw the sad, left-out look on Madison's face.

"I'm sorry," Aimee said. "I should have told you. I forgot. Things are busy since *The Wiz*. . . ."

"You really had lunch with *Ivy*?" Madison said for a second time.

"It's just 'cause of the play, Maddie. We're in the play. You know how it is."

Madison realized she *didn't* know how it was.

From across the auditorium, Mrs. Montefiore and Ivy motioned for Aimee to go over to the piano. Everyone was standing there: Egg, Hart, Fiona, Lindsay . . .

Everyone.

"Why don't you come over too, Maddie?" Aimee said.

Madison thought about it. If she went over to the piano, she'd be right there, crammed together with all the other seventh-grade singers, even Poison Ivy.

Maybe around that crowded piano, she'd really and truly feel like a part of the cast.

Madison put down her stage manager clipboard and started to walk over.

"Uh, Madison," Mr. Gibbons called out. "I need you to run down to the basement and get me some small props. Here's the list. Can you do that for me, please?"

"Right now?" Madison asked.

"Of course. We need to do a little set painting later on, and I want to get things ready. Just ask Mr. Boggs for the key to the basement space. He'll help you."

"But I have to—" Madison started to say, looking over at the piano. Mrs. Montefiore had already started to play.

"Maybe Drew can help you," Mr. Gibbons suggested. "He's up working on the lighting board."

"Forget it," Madison said, walking out of the auditorium. "Just forget it. I'll be fine by myself."

She turned around once at the auditorium doors to look back and see everyone singing at the piano.

Not even Aimee seemed to notice she had gone.

Chapter 7

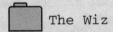 The Wiz

Rude Awakening: Why do they call it a play when it's so much work?

Friday Mr. Gibbons made me go into the hideous dark dungeon that is our school basement. It was like walking into a bad movie. Mr. Boggs, the janitor, wasn't around, so I started looking through boxes on my own.

BIG mistake.

There was a spiderweb near the boiler room that was bigger than my head.

Now, I love animals of all kinds and I don't really mind spiders, either. Most people don't even realize how good spiders are because they eat all the bad bugs. But that web freaked me.

Mr. Gibbons keeps sending me around the school building to get all these things he needs. Most of the time, I bring these "props" up, and the box just gets shoved in the corner of the stage. He isn't even using all of them!!!

I thought being stage manager was important. And fun. But it's mostly just hard work. And I'm running around doing all this stuff like I'm invisible or something while everyone else sings and dances. The show feels like a nightmare sometimes—with the spiders *and* without.

But I didn't give up on the school election Web site, I didn't give up when I fell off a horse at camp two summers ago, and I *won't* give up on *The Wiz*.

Madison couldn't remember a weekend that whizzed by faster than this one. All day Saturday she worked to cross off items on the prop and costume list.

Mom was a huge help. Madison was luckier than lucky to have a mom with connections through Budge Films. Mom called a few friends from a costume company, and they agreed to loan Far Hills some of the more complicated costumes like the Lion suit and the Tin Man's limbs, even in smaller "junior high" sizes.

Saturday night, Mom had to run over to the Tool Box hardware outlet at the mall to buy lightbulbs and a new broom. Madison tagged along.

"Look at all this stuff," Madison said as they walked in the store. Madison's brain nearly blew a fuse when she saw an entire wall with just hammers and spied paint cans piled into pyramids. There was even a special aisle just for nails.

Normally, a hardware store would make Madison say "Boring."

Something was different today. Being stage manager made her think differently.

Against one wall were samples of floor tiles. A sign on one bin read SALVAGED LINOLEUM. Madison plucked out some yellow squares. They glistened when the light hit them the right way.

"Mom," she said. "Do you think we could use these for the yellow brick road?"

Mom gasped. "What a *great* idea, Maddie."

In addition to the tiles, Madison found a bowl that looked like a fortune-teller's crystal ball when you turned it upside down, a tin can for the Tin Man, and a clear plastic rod that could double as a magic wand for Glinda.

"You could decorate that, too," Mom suggested.

"With glitter glue, maybe," Madison said. Every new idea she had was leading to two or three other new ideas.

The Finn living room turned into a prop room once they got home and unpacked the bags.

"Just think, Maddie, two weeks ago you weren't

even going to be a part of the show, and now look." Mom pointed to piles.

Later on, Madison went online to surf the Internet for even more brilliant ideas. Bigfishbowl.com had a search link on its home page. She plugged in some key words to see what interesting sites would turn up.

When Madison entered the word *wizard* into the search engine, it gave her the addresses to an odd assortment of destinations. One link sent Madison to a Wizard of Oz fan club page, while another page linked up to a role-playing game page on magic. She even found the hyperlink for a page on "Muggles Who Like Harry Potter and Other Wizards." She was having so much fun surfing the Net that she lost complete track of time.

More than half the items were crossed off her prop and costume list now. Was she finally mastering this stage manager thing?

Sunday afternoon Madison couldn't wait to tell Dad about all the props. She went over to his place, but they didn't do as much talking as she'd hoped. Madison might be sailing along with work on the show, but she had gotten way behind in her *home*work. Once Dad found that out, he sat her down in his dining room to finish. Dad couldn't believe that Mr. Gibbons would load up his students up with homework during rehearsals for *The Wiz.*

But he had.

She spent two whole hours reading *Diary of Anne Frank* and writing a short essay at Dad's dining room table.

When Monday morning rolled around, Madison was *still* working on her diary assignment. She'd just about finished when Mom asked her to help load the car to bring the yellow brick road tiles and other props to school.

"I'm sooooo stressed out!" Madison said as they motored over to Far Hills. Rushing in the mornings usually meant rushing all day long, too. She would be a little late to Mrs. Wing's first-period computer class.

Luckily Mom had written an excuse note. Mrs. Wing was cool about the whole thing. Mrs. Wing was usually cool about everything.

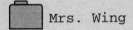 Mrs. Wing

My English essay is DONE! I feel so happy being in computer class now. Not just because I get my work done so much faster than everyone else and can go into my own files like now, but because of my teacher. Being around Mrs. Wing just makes me feel smarter.

Great news! Mrs. Wing told me at the start of class that she would help me make the programs for *The Wiz*. I told her I wanted to design the cover. It'll be like making a collage, and I love making collages. I never know when I start, what words and pictures will end up together. Mrs. Wing couldn't believe it when I told her I kept all my files on the computer and off. She says we can scan the collage at school and then print out final copies for the copy center.

We started talking about *The Wiz* page for the seventh-grade Web site. Mrs. Wing says she'll post pictures online after the show ends. When rehearsals end, I'll be working more on the Web pages in my free time. Principal Bernard told Mrs. Wing he wants Far Hills to be tech connected. (That's what he calls it, anyway.) So next semester we'll be doing more "cybrarian" work, like logging information and making homework databases.

Mrs. Wing had on the most excellent scarf with orange polka dots today, and she doesn't even know that's my favorite color! Mom would say that's good karma. She believes that

"What are you writing?" Egg asked.

Madison clicked off her monitor. He was giving her the evil eye.

"Nothing," Madison said. "Nothing . . . except an e-mail to Rose saying you think she's HOT."

"You what?" Egg said.

"Shhh!" Madison warned. She didn't want to get in trouble. Luckily Mrs. Wing hadn't heard or seen them. "Egg, I was kidding. Relax."

"Tell me what you wrote NOW," Egg said. He gave Madison an Indian sunburn by grabbing her forearm with both hands and *twisting*. . . .

"Owwwwch," Madison squeaked. She looked down at her now beet-red forearm. "That hurt."

The bell rang and Drew walked over to Madison and Egg.

"Are *you* singing today, Tin Boy?" Drew asked.

"Hey, quit the Tin Boy jokes," Egg said. "I'm working on dance steps with Aimee, I think."

"How's Aimee doing with all that?" Madison asked. "I haven't really seen much of her choreography."

"She's wicked bossy," Egg huffed.

"She is not," Madison defended her.

"All girls are bossy," Egg shot back.

"I'm going to tell your sister you said that." Madison pinched him.

"Like she would even care," Egg said, rolling his eyes.

The boys hustled out of the computer lab with Madison behind them. She was on her way to see Egg's sister at that very moment.

Mariah and Madison had been excused from their second-period classes so they could meet about the play. It wasn't a big deal since Madison's second period was Mr. Gibbons. He said she could make up the work later. Mariah had her second period free.

Madison couldn't wait to tell Mariah how she and Mom had collected so many key props over the weekend.

She was prouder than proud.

"Buenos días!" Mariah said when they met up in the newspaper room.

"Buenos días," Madison answered back. "I love the new hair color."

Mariah had painted streaks of red all over her head. She liked to change the color just enough so she made an impression—but didn't get sent to Principal Bernard's office. In addition to a dress code, Far Hills Junior High had rules about dyed hair, pierced body parts, and even tattoos. The rule was: DON'T. One time Mariah had a henna tattoo on her shoulder and she'd been sent home to change into a shirt with longer sleeves.

"It's fuchsia, actually." Mariah ran her fingers through her hair. "Madison, you would look awesome with blue—or maybe even green streaks. Ya wanna try?"

Madison chuckled. "Uh . . . NO."

She was daring with her ideas, but when it came to her hair, Madison wasn't brave at all. She didn't even like getting a haircut.

"I have to meet with the eighth-grade prop person at the end of this period, so we better hurry." Because she was president of the junior high art club, Mariah had extra responsibilities. She was always doing extra work for the club, for shows, and for teachers she liked. Sort of like how Madison felt about Mrs. Wing.

"Okay, let's start." Madison pulled out her list and named all the things she was able to gather.

"Check you out," Mariah said. "Art club is painting the set backdrop after school today. I got four teachers to help and the shop teacher volunteered, too. Did I tell you? We're painting it to look like Broadway. A New York City skyline."

The tribute to Mrs. B. Goode would last three separate evenings, but they'd use the same backdrop for all three shows. The first performance was *The Wiz* selections. The following night, the eighth grade was doing selections from *Guys and Dolls*. The next night would be the ninth grade doing a medley of New York City tunes. Madison was pleased since a city backdrop made an ideal Emerald City.

"You're so good at this," Madison said. "And you're so good at being an artist."

"Well, I don't know about *that*." Mariah smiled. She pointed to her head. "I mean, I do paint my *hair*. You're artistic, too, you know."

Madison blushed.

"Anything bizarre happen at rehearsals yet?"

"Well . . ." Madison said softly. "Rehearsals are fine."

"Come on. What's the matter?"

"Oh, nothing. I'm just not used to it, that's all."

"Used to what?"

"Well, sometimes I don't really feel like *I'm* a part of the show. I know I'm helping, but I still feel so helpless. Like every time we're at rehearsal, Mr. Gibbons makes me go down to get something in the basement or tells me to go deliver papers to the administrator or has me sit and prompt lines all by myself in the audience. Meanwhile everybody else is goofing around and having a great time."

"Being stage manager is hard," Mariah said. "People think it's way harder to stand up onstage and sing a song—"

"It *is* hard to get up onstage and sing," Madison chimed in. "I know I get all panicky whenever I try to do that."

"Yeah, but it's still not as hard as what we do, right? Like planning costumes and making sure all the set pieces are where they should be. Where would Mr. Gibbons be without us doing all this?"

"It just makes me feel . . ." Madison wasn't sure how to say it. "I feel so out of it."

"I hear ya. Kids in my class think I'm out of it, too, just because of the way I dress—" Mariah joked.

"But you dress great," Madison interrupted.

"Yeah, whatever." Mariah shrugged it off. "The point is, they don't get it."

"Get what?"

"*It!* Wait until you get to be a freshman like me. Then it really starts to stink. You never know what's happening. You're like the oldest in some ways, but then you're the youngest in other ways."

Even though she was only two years ahead, Madison really looked up to Mariah. But was it really going to get *worse* as she went along in junior high?

Madison did NOT want to believe it.

"No matter what happens during the show," Mariah said as she walked out, "just remember this. It'll all go back to the way it was when the show ends. So don't stress about the jerks. Like my brother." She winked.

Madison sighed.

"Look, Madison, you're the glue, right?" Mariah said.

Madison gave her a blank look. *The glue?*

"Think of it like this," Mariah tried to explain. "You're the one holding *The Wiz* together, okay? So you're the glue."

It sort of made sense. Mariah's words repeated like a recorded message inside Madison's head.

You're the glue. You're the one holding it together.

Whenever rehearsals felt bizarre or she felt out of it, Madison could take that message and play it again.

Maybe being the glue could be her secret weapon against Poison Ivy?

Maybe it could even get Hart to notice her more?

That night, Madison wanted to talk about *The*

Wiz and "being the glue." Madison didn't like how important ideas could happen when there was no one to share them with.

Mom was under a deadline, so she wasn't talking much.

Aimee and her brothers were off at some family dinner in another town.

Fiona's line was busy.

Madison checked her e-mailbox. She'd been unlucky in e-mail lately, but every time she opened it anew, she held her breath for an extra beat—just in case. It had been a few days since she'd checked. Madison didn't like the idea of deleting messages even if they meant nothing. But she had to eliminate some things.

	FROM	SUBJECT
✉	Wetwins	Surfing the Net Games
✉	Boop-Dee-Doop	Spring Clothes ALL NEW
✉	JeffFinn	Fw: FW: This is so funny!!!
✉	Webmaster@bigfis	discussion boards working
✉	Postmaster	Nondeliverable mail

Nothing in her mailbox made Madison feel any more "with it" than she'd felt hanging with Mariah at rehearsal. It was all e-junk, mostly.

There was a super T-shirt sale at one of her favorite online stores. *Nah.* DELETE.

Dad sent a lame joke about a duck. DELETE.

Fiona's brother, Chet, had written about a Net newsletter he wanted to create, reviewing Web sites and computer games he liked. *Not into it right now, maybe later.* DELETE.

Bigfishbowl was starting up a new area of bulletin boards where kids could safely post messages. *Worth checking out.* SAVE.

Finally Madison saw an e-mail that was returned to her. She had originally sent it to Bigwheels last week. Even worse than getting no e-mail was learning that e-mail you sent didn't arrive.

Madison would have to write another e-mail to Bigwheels right away.

Maybe *this* one would get delivered.

Chapter 8

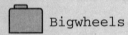 Bigwheels

So I sent Bigwheels this long, long, long e-mail that started out talking about boys and school and ended up talking about how I felt when Mom and Dad had the Big D.

Funny how that subject always comes up, isn't it?

Bigwheels is feeling bad and I hope I can be helpful. So she IMed me back right away and we went to GOFISHY for a chat. I thought, here is the moment when I could make even more of a difference. Yes!

But she left in the middle of talking! She hasn't e-mailed me again, she hasn't IMed me either.

Do I give terrible advice?

Maybe having a friend online isn't the

same as having a *real* friend. Is that why I can't help her? Is Bigwheels a real friend?

Madison got to the lunchroom later than usual Tuesday afternoon.

Gilda Z slopped sloppy joes onto soft buns.

"Cheese or no cheese?" Gilda asked.

Madison placed her tray on the counter. "No cheese, please," she said, and moved along down the line with her plain sloppy joe. They were all out of strawberry yogurts, so she got banilla instead— vanilla and banana mixed. She'd missed *all* the good lunch selections.

After paying for her food, Madison turned into the noisy cafeteria and inspected the room for her friends. She started back toward the orange table in the rear. To her surprise, all her friends were sitting there.

Plus Ivy, Rose, and Joanie.

Madison almost dropped her tray.

"Maddie, over here!" Fiona chirped, shoving over so Madison could sit down. But there wasn't any room on that side. All the boys were on that side. Madison walked around to the other end of the table.

There wasn't any room there, either.

"I guess I'll sit over there," Madison said, moving toward a green table behind the orange one where everyone else was sitting.

Aimee quickly stood up. "No! Maddie, you can

fit! Ivy, can you move down a little? You too, Rose."

Ivy and Rose both pushed their trays down and made room so Madison could sit next to Aimee. They didn't do it quietly, but they moved. Down at the other end, Egg, Drew, Chet, Hart, and Dan, the kid who was playing the Lion, were too busy playing spitball hockey to even look up.

Never in her life did Madison imagine she'd be sitting at the orange table in the back of the room between her best friend and best enemy. But as her gramma Helen always told her, "Never say never to anything."

"Where were you?" Aimee asked. "Why are you late for lunch?"

Madison shrugged. "I had to help Mrs. Wing."

Ivy interrupted. "She's that computer teacher, right?"

Madison nodded and snapped open her yogurt top.

"That's nice for you, I guess . . ." Ivy said. She leaned right over Madison's tray to talk to Aimee. "Did I tell you that Mrs. Montefiore said we could go ahead and do a dance with our solo, Aimee?"

"What solo?" Madison asked.

"Oh, our duet," Ivy clarified, sipping a juice. "Didn't you hear us singing it the other day?"

Rose piped up. "It'll be the best number in the whole show, Aimee. Your choreography is really good."

Madison couldn't believe Rose would ever compliment Aimee on her dance, but she did.

"You and Rose and Ivy are all dancing together?" Madison asked.

"Yeah," Aimee replied.

"Well, I'm not really that good," Rose mumbled. "But Aimee's helping me out."

"You are *too* good," Aimee told her.

Madison looked over at Fiona desperately.

Was this really happening?

"Madison, what are *you* working on for the show?" Ivy asked. "I don't see you at rehearsals much."

"I've been busy with stage managing, Ivy," Madison said. She couldn't believe Ivy was sitting *this* close. Madison could tell she was wearing make-up.

"Nooooooooo!"

Across the table, Hart let out a wail. He'd lost his spitball hockey game.

"That wasn't a penalty. Egg, you stink!" he cried.

Everyone stopped talking.

Hart looked around with a bashful smile.

Madison glanced over at Hart for a second and thought she saw him wink. But seventh-grade boys absolutely don't wink, especially not in the middle of lunch with a million people around, do they? Madison wasn't so sure.

The mere thought of Hart winking in her direction

83

made her feel better about being at the table.

Ivy jostled Madison's arm, and the yogurt cup almost tipped onto the sloppy joes.

"Oh, sorry, did I do that?" Ivy said.

Madison wanted to pour banilla on Ivy's head.

"Hey, Ivy," Egg yelled across the table. "We heard a rumor."

Hart spoke up, too. "Yeah, Ivy, we heard a rumor. Are you having the cast party?"

Fiona was spacing out. "I haven't heard anything. Is it true?"

"Well . . ." Ivy said coyly to the boys only. "Maybe."

Madison turned to Poison Ivy. "*You're* having the cast party?"

"Well, my parents said it was okay," Ivy said, flipping her hair. "So I guess the rumor is true. It should be great."

"Cool," Chet said.

"Is it a cast party, Ivy?" Drew asked. "Or is it cast *and* crew?"

"Huh? I don't know," she said. "Cast, I guess. And crew. I haven't really decided."

"Well, it really isn't for you to decide," Madison muttered.

"Excuse me?" Ivy said.

Phony Joanie clucked her tongue. "I think only people who are really in the show are supposed to go to a cast party, like actors and the director."

"That's not true!" Fiona said. "It's for everyone. It's for your family and friends who aren't even in the show if you want it to be."

"Well," Joanie said. "That's not the kind of cast party I've been to."

Madison knew that Phony Joanie had probably never been to a single cast party in her entire life.

"A cast party is for everyone, even people who are behind the scenes," Aimee said, looking right at Madison.

"The crew—I mean, Madison and Drew—can come," Ivy snarled. "If they really want."

She said that like it was the last thing in the world she wanted to happen.

"Hey, does anybody have a dollar I could borrow?" Dan interrupted. "I wanna get another dessert."

"You already had two desserts," Chet said. "Like, slow down, Lion Man."

"I can't help it. I'm hungry," Dan said, grabbing a half-eaten brownie off Chet's tray. "Fine, I'll eat yours, then."

Aimee laughed, but her smile disappeared when she looked over at Madison. "What's that on your shirt?" she whispered.

Madison looked down.

Splat.

The whole time she'd been eating her lunch, her sloppy joe had been slopping. There were orange blotches in three different places.

Rose and Joanie snickered.

"Here." Fiona handed Madison a wet napkin across the table. "You can't even tell that you spilled it."

"I can't believe I just did that," Madison said aloud.

Ivy snickered, too.

"Is something funny?" Madison turned to her.

Ivy held up her hands in front of her face and shook her head as if she hadn't laughed.

"Is something wrong?" Madison asked.

Ivy stood up and grabbed her tray. "Not with me. What about you?"

The boys got up to go when Ivy stood. Madison wondered if they did that on purpose.

Even Hart got up. "Looks like this party is break-ing up," he said, grabbing his backpack.

Egg, Chet, Dan, and Drew followed.

Madison wanted to shout out, "Good-bye, Hart," but it was too late. The boys were halfway out of the cafeteria without turning back.

Ivy and her drones were right behind him.

"*That* was totally awkward," Fiona said to Madison. "Why did you get all weird with Ivy?"

"Because she was being a jerk," Madison said.

Aimee nodded. "I guess. A little."

"You guess? A little? I thought you were my friends," Madison said.

Aimee leaned in. "What are you talking about?"

"If you were my friends, you would not be sitting here at our table with the most popular, most obnoxious, most EVIL people in the school."

"Maddie, it's really not that bad. Why are you acting like this? I mean, it wasn't even a problem having lunch all together—until you came over."

"What's *that* supposed to mean?" Madison said.

"You—you know what I mean," Aimee stammered.

"You just sat there," Madison said. "While she and her drones laughed at me."

Fiona shrugged. "She wasn't *really* laughing, Maddie."

"Then what was *really* happening?" Madison tried in vain to mop away the sloppy joe on her shirt, but the stains just got worse. "What a mess!"

"Maddie, we're your best friends," Aimee explained. "We were just hanging out."

"Whatever," Madison said, wiping some more at the sloppy joe stain.

"Madison, don't you believe us?" Fiona asked.

Madison realized she *did* believe them. They were her best friends. But she was still angry. Really angry.

"I don't mean to be weird." Madison sighed. "It's just that I couldn't believe I would ever find you eating lunch at the same table—at *our* orange table—with Ivy Daly."

"It's just that Ivy has been pretty cool." Aimee

put her arm around her best friend. "About the show, I mean."

Madison was *really* trying to understand.

"She's being so nice to me and Fiona," Aimee said.

She's being so FAKE. Don't you get it?

She wanted to say that out loud but decided not to say anything.

The three friends got up and started to leave.

"Madison, wait!" a voice yelled from the other side of the lunchroom. It was Lindsay Frost. "I have something to ask you," she said.

"Hi, Lindsay," Fiona said.

Aimee waved hello and then said to Madison, "We'll wait over there."

"I'm so glad I caught you!" Lindsay was talking fast. Madison noticed that her hair wasn't combed. She even had a sloppy joe stain on her sweater. It was kind of gross. Madison looked down at her own shirt.

"You spilled lunch, too, huh?" Lindsay smiled, pointing at Madison and then back at herself.

Madison held her hands over her blotches. "No, not really."

Were all eyes in the lunchroom on them?

"Um, did you say you had a question for me?"

"Yes! I was looking for you earlier. I wanted to see if you had time to practice lines with me later," Lindsay said.

88

"Later?" Madison asked.

"Before or after rehearsal, I guess. Or if you have a free period."

"Oh," Madison said. She couldn't take her eye off Lindsay's sloppy joe spot. Did her own shirt look as bad as Lindsay's sweater?

Aimee and Fiona were standing over by the exit doors, waving and waiting.

"Well, can you help?" Lindsay asked again.

"Well," Madison started to answer. She was about to say, "Yeah, sure, yeah, I'll go," but then Aimee make a face. A funny face.

Lindsay was oblivious as usual. Madison wanted to run.

"I'm sorry," Madison blurted out suddenly. "I'd really like to help . . . but I can't. I have so much work for the show and I'm really behind in my classes and maybe we can do it tomorrow?"

"Oh." Lindsay shrugged. "No, that's okay. Don't worry about it. I understand. I'll see you at rehearsal. Another time, I guess."

As Lindsay walked away, Madison hurried over to Aimee and Fiona.

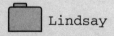 Lindsay

Rude Awakening: Popularity is a war I can't win.

I watch the other kids onstage and I wonder what's real and what's not. People

89

can be such fakers, and when they're singing and acting it's even worse. Even people you thought you knew.

That fakeness just continues right off the stage into life, doesn't it? I should have helped Lindsay today when she asked me. But I didn't. Dissing Lindsay was more embarrassing than spilling sloppy joe on myself in front of Hart and everyone else. It was way more embarrassing than anything I've done lately. How could I be so un-nice?

Even when I think I can rise above the whole mind trip about what's popular and what's not, I *still* get sucked in by what other people think. I care what they think. Does that make me a bad person?

What happened to being the glue and holding everything together like Mariah said? I am so not holding ANYTHING together right now.

I can't figure out where I fit in.

Chapter 9

The morning of the first dress rehearsal, Madison got up extra early to get a head start on some positive vibes. She was up at five-thirty, to be exact. A case of major nerves can sometimes be the best alarm clock in the world.

Phinnie made a snuffling noise and curled into a tighter ball when Madison stretched and slid out from under the covers. But ever so quietly, Madison perched by the bedroom window seat to watch the sun come up like a piece of tangerine candy.

More than anything else in the entire world, Madison wanted to do a good job in *The Wiz*. As she looked out at the sky she made a wish for that . . . times two . . . with sugar on top . . . crossing her fingers just to be sure. Superstitions couldn't be proved; Madison knew that. But they didn't hurt.

"Please don't let me mess up," she said aloud to the sky. "Please don't let me miss any cues or drop any props. Please let *The Wiz* be the best show ever."

By the time the dress rehearsal started, she was readier than ready to watch that wish come true.

"Let's get this show on the road!" Mr. Gibbons yelled. He motioned up to the mezzanine to Drew and Wayne, who were running the lights, to begin. "Is everyone almost ready back there?"

This was the true test. Everyone always says a bad dress rehearsal is good news for the real show. Madison wanted to believe that *both* could be fantastic.

Mariah rushed into the dressing area. "Has anyone seen Toto—I mean, Chocolate?"

Mr. Gibbons had brought in his own dog, Chocolate, to be in the early scenes as Dorothy's dog, Toto. The poor animal had only been at one rehearsal so far and had been so traumatized by the lights and the music that she'd peed onstage.

A low barking noise was coming from behind one of the curtains at the far end of the stage. Mariah heard it first.

"Bad girl, Chocolate!" she exclaimed as she retrieved the mutt from between a heavy fold of fabric. The dog had gotten tangled up back in the curtains and was shaking like a windup toy.

A missing Toto is not a good omen, Madison

thought, crossing her fingers again. She went back into the dressing room.

"Hey, Finnster!" Hart cried as Madison entered the dressing room.

He was decked out in a purple flowing cape and carried his mask in hand. The mask, constructed out of papier-mâché by the ninth-grade art club, was twice the size of Hart's real head. It was more like a monster head really, with giant sunken holes for his eyes and red feathers at the top that looked like flames shooting out. It was attached to a broom handle so Hart could hold it up in front of his face during the early Oz scenes—just before Dorothy and the others discover that The Wizard is a big faker.

Egg was standing nearby. "Hey, Hart, that's a good way to get girls."

"That's real funny, Tin Boy head," Hart said as he held up the mask. "Hey, what do *you* think, Finnster?"

Just as he said that, the mask came detached from its handle.

"Hart!" Madison yelped. She leaned forward and caught it.

"Whoa," Hart said. "That was close. But now what am I supposed to do? Lift it up like this—"

"No, let's fix it." Madison ran over to the prop shelves and retrieved some twine and duct tape that other people in the crew left around just in case anything needed to be tied up or reattached. The mask was repaired instantly.

"Madison, can you help me, too?" Fiona said.

On the other side of the prop closet, Fiona was searching for her witch hat, which had been mysteriously misplaced.

"It was here a little while ago," Madison told her. "I double-checked my entire list. Are you sure you didn't pick it up?"

Fiona looked frazzled. "No, I swear. Well, maybe. Oh, I don't remember. It's so busy back here and—"

"Is someone missing a witch hat?" Mariah said, walking toward Fiona.

Madison breathed a sigh of relief. "Don't take it off, Fiona, okay?"

Fiona really could be the world's biggest space case.

Peeking through the curtains, Madison could see Mr. Gibbons hunched over the piano with Mr. and Mrs. Montefiore. They were reviewing the order of song numbers. Mr. Gibbons had rearranged and shortened the *Wiz* tunes with the music department. For now the piano played, but for the real show, they were adding drums, cymbals, and a trumpet. Those band members just weren't expected at rehearsal today.

Madison had set up a bench with a script on it so she could easily cue missed lines. She saw Ivy leaning over the script, flipping pages to find her parts.

"Ivy, you need to go finish getting dressed," Madison said.

Ivy kept looking through the pages.

Madison moaned. "Why don't you go look at your own script, Ivy? We're starting in a few minutes and I need to—"

"Look, I don't come on for a few songs, so I have plenty of time to get in costume," Ivy said. "And I need to look at this script now. I left mine in my locker."

Madison shook her head. "No." She grabbed the script. "Get dressed."

Ivy looked steamed. Had Madison really said that?

Rose and Joan walked over. They'd heard everything.

"You can use my script, Ivy," Rose said. "I'm not stingy, like some people around here."

The three enemies skulked away.

"How do I look?" Lindsay asked. She modeled her braid-in pigtails and gingham jumper. She was carrying Chocolate in her arms. He was still shaking from the curtain incident.

"You're the perfect Dorothy," Madison said. "That's a great costume."

"Thanks," Lindsay said.

"Do you have everything else you need?" Madison asked.

Lindsay nodded. She stuck out her pinkie.

"What's that for?" Madison asked.

Lindsay smiled. "For luck. I'm very superstitious, aren't you?"

"Hey, Madison." Mariah poked her head out of the dressing room. "I have to help the Munchkins lace up their green shoes, so I'll be back here. Are you okay by yourself?"

Madison smiled. "I think so."

"She's totally in control," Lindsay said as she walked to the other side of the stage for her entrance. "Thanks again, Maddie."

Madison wasn't exactly in total control, even though she wished she were. Frantic cast members had her surrounded. There were other teachers and crew people around, but everyone seemed to need *Madison* to help.

Help!

Tommy's scarecrow stuffing was coming undone. Madison stuffed it in and tied a new knot in his costume to make it all better.

Dan's lion suit was a little too big and he kept stumbling around, bumping into people and things backstage. Madison unzipped his paws and rolled up his leg fur.

"We'll figure it out after rehearsal," she told him. "This will work for now."

"My wand is missing!" Ivy screeched. She practically spit the words into Madison's face. "Aren't you supposed to keep track of the props, Madison?" She said Madison's name like it tasted bad.

"Yes, but you wanted to be in charge of your own props, remember?" Madison reminded Ivy that she was the one who didn't want anyone near any part of her costume. She'd made that perfectly clear during rehearsals, so Mr. Gibbons told her she could keep her stuff separate from the rest of the cast's as long as she kept track of it.

"But you're the prop person and you're supposed to know what to do, right?" Ivy snarled.

"I do know what to do," Madison said. She walked away, leaving Ivy there alone in her Glinda outfit with an expression of utter disbelief.

"I'm going to tell Mr. Gibbons," Ivy threatened.

Madison didn't care. "Have you seen Aimee?" she asked Mariah.

Five Munchkins looked up at Madison and pointed toward the backstage bathroom.

"Aimee?" Madison called out. "Are you in there?"

A muffled voice from behind the door squeaked, "Yes."

It was Aimee, but she didn't sound like herself.

"Aimee? Are you okay?" Madison rattled the knob. "Can I come in?"

The door unlatched and Madison walked inside. Aimee was leaning up against the sink.

"Aimee, what's the matter?" Madison asked. They were looking at each other in the mirror reflection.

Aimee shook her head. "I have cramps. Bad ones."

Madison rubbed her back. "Did you eat something weird for lunch?"

"Not those kind of cramps." Aimee lowered her voice so Madison could barely hear. "I have my period."

Madison didn't know what to say. She and Aimee had never really talked about this. Madison hadn't gotten hers yet.

"What should I do?" Aimee asked.

"You want me to tell Mrs. Montefiore that you have your period?" Madison asked.

"Noooo! Don't tell anyone," Aimee said. "I'll be okay. I better just get into my costume."

"Are you sure?" Madison asked.

Aimee put down the toilet seat and sat. She grabbed at her stomach and took a deep breath. "Cramp," she whispered.

"Aimee?" Madison was worried.

But a heartbeat later, Aimee stood right back up. "I'm fine. They come and go, you know?"

Madison realized she *didn't* know. Not one bit. She was eager to get older and wiser, but Madison could definitely wait for her period. She wasn't ready to enter the world of cramps.

"Aimee, are you nervous, too?" Madison asked before walking out.

"I don't get nervous. I don't get all weird when I

have to go onstage. I go onstage all the time at dance camp. Why would right now be any different than then? I just think—"

Aimee paused and took a deep, deep breath.

"I've never been so nervous, Maddie," Aimee finally admitted. "I don't want to mess up. All those dance steps and—"

"Aimee, you'll be great," Madison said. "You know you'll be great. You always dance great, no matter what. Even with cramps.'"

Aimee looked straight into Madison's eyes. "You're the best."

"The Munchkins are waiting," Madison joked.

As she walked out of the girls' bathroom, Madison was so lost in thought that she almost smacked right into Tommy Kwong. Once again, he'd come unstuffed. Madison restuffed.

"Madison!" Mariah yelled. "There's someone outside from the local paper. They want to take a picture of everyone in the show. Mr. Gibbons wants you and everyone else on the stage."

Sometimes the local paper ran human-interest stories about school events like this. This article was going to be about Mrs. Goode's twenty years at the school and her various contributions to the Far Hills community. They wanted photos from a dress rehearsal so they could run the piece the day of the show. They'd be doing separate pieces on the seventh-, eighth-, and ninth-grade performances.

Mr. Gibbons had turned up the house lights. "Uh, can I get everyone out here, please? All the seventh-grade cast members onstage."

The Montefiores stopped playing. Madison and Mariah helped to corral the witches and Winkies onto the set. They were standing in front of the city backdrop, and it looked so magical. The yellow linoleum squares twinkled when the lights hit them in just the right way.

"Okay, now let's line up," Mr. Gibbons asked the cast.

Amazingly, everyone got into rows and the photographer asked everyone to stand closer. Madison crossed her arms and watched everyone come together. It was so exciting!

Fiona waved her over.

"Here," Fiona said. "Get in the picture! Stand next to me!"

Aimee put her arm around Madison's shoulder when she slipped in.

"Hold on!" the photographer yelled. "Would the Tin Man please straighten his tin hat?"

Egg fixed it.

"No, no—I need the Munchkins to be in the same group, please," he said raising his camera up to his eye again. "Yes, that's better."

Mr. Gibbons yelled out, "Dan, would you please roll down your lion feet?"

Madison helped.

"Okay." The photographer made little hand motions to tell kids to move in, move out, and then move in again. "Would the boy playing the Scarecrow please check his straw?"

Madison looked over at Tommy. Mrs. Perez needed to work on that costume a little more.

"Okay, now everyone smile," the photographer said, lifting the camera up once more.

Mr. Gibbons suddenly stepped in front of the camera. "Wait! Ivy Daly isn't here. Ivy? How could we be missing Ivy?" he yelled backstage. "Madison, where did Ivy go?"

"I'll get her," Mariah said, running to the back. Madison was very glad she didn't have to go.

In a second, Ivy was onstage, apologizing. She had *finally* found her Glinda wand.

"Now are we ready?" the photographer asked once more.

Everyone smiled.

"Wait! I'm sorry, but who is the girl in the second row? The one in between the two witches?"

Madison knew he was talking about her.

"She's our stage manager," Mr. Gibbons said.

"Could I ask you to please step out of the picture, miss? This is just for cast members wearing costumes."

Madison felt everyone's eyes on her. "It's okay, Madison," Mr. Gibbons reassured her. "You can be in the next round of photos."

Madison slowly walked to the side of the stage.

"Thanks!" the photographer cried. "Now, *Wiz* cast, please say 'Oz!'"

Madison blinked when the flash went off and got dizzy. The photographer kept taking picture after picture, posing the group in different arrangements. He even took shots of Addaperle, Evillene, and Glinda by themselves. The three of them looked great in their costumes.

By the time Madison got into the photo, the photographer only had a few shots left. She posed with Drew and the Nose Plucker. Madison knew *she* wouldn't make the paper, but she tried not to let it bother her. The cast and crew photo might make it into one of the trophy cases in the school lobby.

When the picture-taking hubbub died down, the cast finally started their opening number. The actual dress rehearsal took about twice as long as it should have, but it finally ended around six-thirty, to loud applause from Mr. Gibbons. He gathered everyone onstage for a little postperformance pep talk.

"You guys were great," he said. "See you back here on Monday."

"That's it?" Egg said.

Mr. Gibbons nodded. "That's it. Good job. Now get your gear and get home." Because it had gotten late, he kept it real short.

Kids were pulling off their costumes in a hurry, so Madison and Mariah kept running from place to place backstage. They had to make sure that props were returned, capes were hung up, and all the caps to the makeup tubes were twisted on tight.

When she was finished running around, Madison had lost track of Aimee and Fiona. They weren't in the dressing room, the bathroom, or the auditorium.

"Have you seen Aimee?" Madison asked Dan.

He played dumb and put on his Lion voice. "Duh, which way did dey go?"

Madison laughed as she walked away. Dan was a dork, but he was funny.

She bumped into Lindsay at the auditorium entrance.

"Hey, did you see Aimee or anyone else?" Madison asked her.

"Nope," Lindsay began. "Yeah! I did see Aimee. She was headed out with her stuff like five minutes ago. Fiona was with her, I think."

Madison sighed. *They'd left without her?*

"You know, Madison, you really should have been in those photographs," Lindsay said. "I mean, you're the most important person in the show."

"Yeah, well . . ." Madison mumbled. "No biggie."

"Still, I hope you know how psyched we all are. Everyone thinks you're a great stage manager."

Madison scratched her head. "Thanks."

"I mean it," Lindsay said.

"That's really nice of you to say that," Madison said. "I mean, you don't have to."

"I know. So you wanna walk home together?" Lindsay asked her.

Just then, Aimee ran into the auditorium. "Oh my God, Maddie! I felt a little sick and I went down to the nurse's office to see if anyone was there. I'm so sorry, but I couldn't find you! Fiona's waiting outside. My brother is coming with the car."

Lindsay started to walk away. "I'll see you guys later, then."

Madison looked at Lindsay and then Aimee and then over at Lindsay again. "Want a ride?" she asked.

Aimee jumped in."Yeah, come with us."

Lindsay looked at Aimee. "You sure?"

Aimee smiled. "Of course, I'm sure."

Madison turned to Lindsay. "Come on, let's go."

Chapter 10

From: Bigwheels
To: MadFinn
Subject: Hi
Date: Sat 14 Oct 10:15 PM

Thanks for sending a copy of your school program cover for *The Wiz*. I downloaded it and it looks so cool.

I am feeling ok now. My mom and dad are seeing a counselor I think. I guess I have to wait and see what happens. The only problem is that I can't get all my homework done and I'm worried about my grades. Do you study hard? I just have so much more homework than I had last year. I think teachers believe in cruel and unusual punishment. My brain hurts.

Send me more e-mails about the play. How is the guy playing The Wizard? Do you still like him? Thanks again for being my keypal and for your advice. It's nice having you out there.

Yours till the home works,

Bigwheels

Even Bigwheels had trouble at school. It was just another thing they had in common. She sounded like she was in better spirits since her last e-mail. Maybe Madison really did help her keypal. Maybe she should make Bigwheels her own special collage about being smart. Bigwheels said she liked the *Wiz* cover, which meant she'd probably *love* a collage of her own.

Madison rummaged through the piles on her floor for the right words and pictures. She found a cartoon of a computer and some pictures of flowers her mom had taken in Thailand on a business trip a while ago.

It was nice to take a break from all things related to *The Wiz*.

The house was so quiet. Mom was out running errands and then taking Phinnie to the vet for his regular checkup. Madison almost never missed Phin's trip to the vet, but she made an exception this once.

Mom said it was okay for her to sleep in after the busy week.

Madison thought about staying under the covers. But she wasn't about to waste valuable time alone—*sleeping*.

She turned the stereo volume in the living room to its highest setting. She could feel the bass vibrate inside the wood floors as the radio played America's Top 40. As her frozen waffles popped out of the toaster, Madison sang along even though she couldn't sing. She liked the part of the radio show where people called from all over the country to dedicate songs to people they loved. One day Madison would call with her own song request. She'd dedicate her song to Hart.

When the radio show ended, she went into Mom's office to boot up her computer. This was the best part about being alone in the house. She could sit at Mom's workstation and imagine that *she*, Madison, was the real-life film producer. She was Madison Finn—making an important call, dashing off a quick memo, taking a meeting.

Madison loved the idea of being important.

She also liked the idea of being just a *little* sneaky.

Mom didn't like it when Madison played video games, so she had strict rules about computer game time and kept all the games on the shelf in her office. But with Mom gone, Madison could play. Today she installed Troll Village, the not-yet-released video game software Mom got from someone at Budge Films.

In Troll Village, Madison had to trick all the trolls in the town in order to become sheriff and rule the area. It was like the Wild, Wild West with saloons and horse stables, only the gunslingers weren't wearing cowboy hats. They had pink, blue, and neon yellow troll hair. Madison could sit and play for almost an hour without moving a muscle. She wasn't sure she even blinked when she played.

When the phone rang, Madison jumped so suddenly that she pressed the mouse accidentally and eliminated one of her troll's seven lives.

Whoops.

"Hello, Finn residence." She answered the phone in a special way just in case it was a work-related call for Mom.

There was silence on the other end of the line.

"Hello, is somebody there? Who is this?" Madison knew *someone* was on the line.

"Maddie, is that you?" It was Drew Maxwell.

"Drew?" Madison asked. "Is that *you*?"

"Yeah. What's up?"

"Um . . . not much."

Madison took the game off pause and played while she talked on the phone.

"How's your weekend?" Drew asked.

"Um . . . fine." Madison had no idea why he'd be calling her.

"I didn't see you after the rehearsal. I wanted to tell you that all your stuff looked good."

"Uh-huh." Madison was half listening now.

"What do you think about the lighting?" Drew asked.

Madison had turned back to her trolls, so she didn't really hear.

"Maddie, are you there?" Drew asked again. "Did you like what we did with the footlights?"

"Yeah," Madison mumbled. "Oh, sure."

She couldn't get the least bit excited about talking to Drew. Ever since they'd been helping Mrs. Wing out with the Web site at school, Drew had been hanging around Madison nonstop. She felt bad because he wasn't always sure what to say. She was half afraid he might say something mushy.

There was nothing worse than the vacuum of silence on the phone between them. Like now.

Drew coughed.

Madison coughed.

"So, anyway," Madison said. "I sorta have to go."

Drew gulped. "Are you coming over today to watch the movie?"

"The movie?" Madison didn't know about any movie.

"Yeah, the movie."

"What movie? Where?"

"At my parents' guest house. We're renting the original *Wizard of Oz* and everyone's coming over to watch it."

Madison was confused. "Everyone? Like who?"

"From the play," Drew said. "We said we'd watch the movie, remember? You were there."

"No, I don't think so."

"You don't know about the movie?"

"No," Madison said again. "No one told me there was a movie." She was repeating herself like a parrot.

"Whoa," Drew moaned. "I guess Fiona forgot to tell you. She told me she'd ask you. I think. Yeah. We were talking about renting the movie the other day, and then I asked my mom if we could do it because we have that big-screen TV. You know the one in the guest house?"

"Uh-huh." Madison felt the exact same way she felt in first grade when she was the only person in class who wasn't invited to Willie Walker's birthday party. Mrs. Walker said the invitation had gotten lost in the mail, but Madison never believed it.

Drew was still talking. "And so everyone just sort of invited themselves. Egg has a big mouth—you know that."

"Uh-huh." Madison grunted. *So why hadn't Egg told her?*

"I guess we forgot to ask you."

"I guess." Madison grunted again.

"But you were *always* totally invited."

"Why didn't you ask me yourself?" Madison asked. "I mean, we only see each other all the time these days at the play and in computer class, too."

"Uh—uh—uh . . . I know. . . . B-B-But . . ." Drew was stammering a lot now. He did that when he got real nervous. "I'm SORRY," he said. "I swear I thought one of the girls was gonna ask you. Fiona said she would. I SWEAR."

"What time does it start?" Madison asked.

"Three," Drew said. "Well, can you come?" he asked. "I mean, now that you know?"

"I have one question," Madison said. "Will Ivy Daly be there?"

"I don't think so," Drew said.

When Drew confirmed that Ivy would *not* be at the screening, Madison agreed to come over—no problem, no hard feelings attached.

Drew sounded relieved when he said good-bye. Madison was relieved, too, that the conversation was over.

As she hung up the phone, she felt freakier than freaky. Mom and the dog walked in the moment she put down the receiver.

"Grrr . . ." Phinnie nuzzled Madison's foot.

"Will you take him for a *w-a-l-k*, please?" Mom asked as she kissed Madison hello.

"Wanna go out?" Madison asked. Phin panted as she grabbed the leash and raced him to the door. Of course, Phinnie won—sliding to the finish. Whenever he ran anywhere too fast in the house, he'd skid across the polished floors.

Madison walked around the block in a trance. She was trying to remember everything in her closet, row by row. She had no idea what she was going to wear to Drew's place. Once she changed out of her sweatpants and oversized T-shirt from her dad's alma mater, she had to put on something cute. Boys were going to be there. Hart was going to be there.

"Will his mother be home?" Mom asked Madison when she came back from the walk. Mom didn't like Madison going places without chaperones.

"I think . . ." Madison suddenly worried that Mom might not agree to let her go. She considered lying, but then admitted she really wasn't sure. "I think so," Madison said again, wishful.

Mom finally said that Madison could go.

"Thanks, Mom. This could be a very important movie, you know."

"Okay, honey bear," Mom said with a nod. "Now go change. It's after two-thirty."

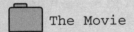 The Movie

I was the last person to get there.

It's weird to (1) not get invited in the first place and then (2) walk in when everyone else has already been there for a while. It's like I had a neon sign on my head that said, "By the Way, I Was Invited at the Last Minute."

I always have over-thoughts—today I was the afterthought.

Right away Aimee and Fiona made room for me between them on the floor, so it got better. Plus Fiona said it was all her fault for not asking me. She just spaced. After that it was pretty much normal for a while. Egg wouldn't shut up; Drew was being Mr. Nice as always. His mom made all this popcorn and it was *everywhere* on the floor.

And then the doorbell rang. Of course it was Ivy. She decided to come at the last minute. Drew was nice to her, too. All the boys were. She was wearing this shirt that was way too tight and jeans that were too tight, too.

I could almost pretend she wasn't there if I sat with my back to her. But when we paused the tape for snack break, Aimee got up to go talk to her. I couldn't believe that! Even Fiona thought that was a little weird.

Hart wasn't there. I wonder why? Lindsay wasn't there, either. I guess no one remembered to invite her, either.

It's bad enough that Ivy has to win things like elections and play parts, but suddenly it's like she has to win *people*, too. When she and Aimee started singing their duet just for fun, I wanted to RUN.

Tonight when I see Dad for dinner, I know he'll say I'm over-thinking this whole Ivy thing. After all, it is just one play. But what if this isn't a temporary thing? Aimee's brothers all told her there are

MAJOR changes in seventh grade. What if changing *friends* is one of them?

But how do you just *forget* to invite your BFF to the movies?

After feeling snubbed at Drew's, the last thing Madison was prepared to deal with was Dad's girlfriend, Stephanie. But Dad invited her along for dinner, despite Madison's protests.

"I want you to be nice," Dad pleaded. "Please."

Madison tried. Dad seemed so blissed out when he was around Stephanie. He smiled nonstop and made even more dumb jokes than usual.

And Madison had to admit, Stephanie really was nice. It was just hard to see another person sitting across the table from Dad where Mom used to sit.

At dinner, Stephanie told Madison how she'd been an actress all through college. She was so enthusiastic, which took Madison by surprise.

"You were?" Madison asked.

Stephanie nodded. "I think being in a show is a terrific way to find out more about yourself. When you act, you can become anyone or anything."

"And what about being offstage?" Madison asked. "Being a stage manager?"

"Well." Stephanie leaned in a little closer to Madison and whispered, "Then you're in charge—of you, of the cast, of everything."

Madison noticed Dad's expression as he looked at

Stephanie. His eyes were shiny like wet marbles. He couldn't stop staring.

It was embarrassing.

Madison didn't remember if Dad ever looked at Mom that way. She tried to search her memory banks like she searched on the Internet, thinking of specific "search" words to see if they'd trigger any memories: *love, dinner, kiss.*

But she came up empty. *No matches found.*

That night before bed, Madison fished through her piles of files, pictures, and words about theater, acting, taking charge. She thought maybe she could make Stephanie a collage, too?

She'd do one for Bigwheels first . . . then one for Stephanie.

Madison shut her eyes tight. What she really needed was sleep.

The play was only days away.

Chapter 11

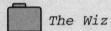 *The Wiz*

I learned how to sew a cape. Actually, I sewed part of Hart's cape. Mrs. Perez really sewed most of it. But still, it's like a part of me will be with him during the show. How cool is *that*?

Tuesday. Boring. I am so busy, I barely have time to write. I have like two hours of homework and it's ten o'clock already. We had another dress rehearsal today. It was forty-eight minutes exactly. Didn't stop for anyone. One funny part was when Ivy forgot her line in one of the songs and I had to cue her. She was MAD about that.

Thursday. Wow. Final run-through. We cleaned the stage afterward. Aimee's dances are so great. It's better that Rose is in the dance numbers because when they dance side by side, Aimee blows her away. Aimee has been so busy practicing, we haven't really talked. Fiona has a cold, but it actually makes the bad-witch voice better. Egg is good, too. We're all GREAT! *The Wiz* is GREAT!!!!

On Friday, Madison logged online before breakfast. With *The Wiz* on the horizon, she was feeling ultrasuperstitious. She decided to go to bigfishbowl.com for a little help. Just before every major life event Madison would visit "Ask the Blowfish" on her favorite Web site.

Right now was no exception.

Site members were instructed to ask a yes or no question on-screen, directing their question to an all-knowing blowfish that looked like a puffy gumball with fins. When she typed her question and hit ENTER, a bubble popped up with the answer. The answers were like wacko fortune cookie fortunes, and Madison knew the way the answers appeared was random, but she believed them, anyway.

She wanted to believe.

Madison typed: *Will the play be good tonight?*

The fish blew a bubble with its answer. "Things will go swimmingly."

Madison was very encouraged.

Will everyone like the show?

The fish said, "The tide is high."

Madison was still encouraged. She had to ask the next question.

Will Hart talk to me tonight?

The fish said, "Beware of sharks."

Madison couldn't believe a blowfish could possibly be SO right. It was like the computer knew about Poison Ivy. *She* was the shark, after all.

Madison asked one more question.

Does Hart like me?

The fish said, "The tide is high."

Madison was thrilled to hear that . . . but then she realized that the blowfish already gave that answer once.

"But it's still a positive," she told herself.

She checked her mailbox, too, while she was online and found an electronic card waiting there. It was better news than what the blowfish delivered. On it was a picture of some kind of cartoon wizard.

```
Make a Wish
You're a "wiz" at whatever you do!
Thought this was funny! Hope every-
thing goes well backstage. Write
soon.
Yours till the leg breaks,

Bigwheels
```

Madison closed her laptop and went down to the kitchen. She'd hang with Phinnie while she ate her cereal. When she'd finished eating, Madison got down on the floor beside him and rubbed his belly. Phin was snoring, curled up by the dishwasher. His shallow little breaths were so peaceful.

Dogs have a way of telling a person everything will be okay just by lying there. Madison read somewhere that dogs never forget. Even if someone is gone for a year, once he or she comes back, that dog will sniff and love and be a friend just like before. When a dog does that, people know they're home.

"I have to go, Maddie! Do you want a lift to school?" Mom said, walking into the kitchen.

Madison couldn't pass up a ride this morning. It was raining.

Was rain a good omen or a bad one?

"We're off to see *The Wizard*," Mom joked as they pulled out of the driveway.

When Mom said, "Wizard," all Madison could think of was Hart.

Everyone in homeroom cheered when Mr. Bernard made his morning announcements about the show.

"To all the students at Far Hills who are participating in the revues from classes seven through nine, thanks for all your hard work. You have made this a very special week, especially for Mrs. Goode, who has devoted much of her teaching career to helping Far Hills students. I ask that all teachers and counselors please take into consideration that students who are participating in the show be given special . . ."

Listening, Madison felt better instantly. She wouldn't stress about her work right now. She couldn't. She had to concentrate on the play.

It would have been nice if Madison's science teacher, Mr. Danehy, had been in agreement with Principal Bernard. While the majority of the seventh-graders could think of nothing else except *The Wiz*, Mr. Danehy thought it was important for the seventh graders to be thinking about tsunamis and sound waves.

During last period, he announced a science test out of the blue—on waves of all kinds.

"Test Monday. No exceptions," he said, stepping into the science storage closet for a moment. No one, not even Hart, was ready for a test.

When Mr. Danehy was out of sight, Chet stood at the front of the room and suggested that they go into his desk to steal the test so everyone could get an A and make Mr. Danehy bonkers. Egg thought that was a great idea, too. But Madison reminded them both that they probably didn't want to get caught and be expelled, right?

"Expelled?" Egg said.

"Hey, I was only kidding," Chet said.

When Mr. Danehy reentered the class, the students pleaded for mercy in rounds like "Row, Row, Row Your Boat."

"Please, please, change the date?"

"Mr. Danehy, we have play practice."

"*The Wiz* is over soon."

"Well," Mr. Danehy said, standing in the back of the class with his arms folded against his chest. "I see."

Everyone breathed a sigh of hope when he said he would *think* about changing the test date. Thinking about it was better than nothing.

Two hours before the show was supposed to go on, before anyone had on costume or makeup, *The Wiz* cast and crew gathered together backstage. Mariah and Wayne were there, too. It was pep talk time. Mr. Gibbons had something very important to tell everyone.

"So here it is, kids," he started out. "The moment we've all be waiting for, right? *The Wiz* is here."

"Yes, I am, Mr. Gibbons," Hart called out. "I'm right over here."

That got a big, nervous laugh.

"We had only a short time to pull together and do this, cast—"

Drew interrupted. "And crew, Mr. Gibbons. Don't forget."

"Yes, Drew, cast *and* crew. And I am wowed by how well you all worked together as a group."

Madison looked over at Aimee, who was sitting to her left, across the room at Ivy, and then over by the door at Lindsay.

Fiona leaned over to the right and whispered in Madison's ear, "Are you nervous?"

"Big time," Madison whispered back. "Are you?"

"Big time." Fiona stuck her arm inside Madison's. "Remember when you told me not to be nervous? That day when the cast was posted?"

They looked over at Aimee together and she pointed to Mr. Gibbons, who wasn't looking in their direction at the time. He was talking too much tonight. He must be nervous, too.

Aimee made a goofy face like she was pretending to scream silently. "Help me!" she mouthed the words. Madison and Fiona almost lost it when she did that.

"So, kids." Mr. Gibbons turned back toward them. "When you get inside the auditorium, there will be lots of activity. We're the class leading off the program, and that's a big responsibility. I want you to be careful, pay attention . . . and HAVE FUN."

He turned to Mrs. Montefiore, who had a few words to say. "I will lead vocal warm-ups backstage. After which everyone can get dressed and ready to go. Understood?"

Everyone nodded.

Ivy raised her hand and talked at the same time. "Do we come out for standing ovations? How do we line up for our curtain call?"

"That's assuming people are clapping." Mr. Gibbons laughed.

Good one, Mr. Gibbons.

"Actually that's a good question, Ivy. You'll get applause after each of your songs. And for the final number, you'll all stay in place and take one last bow."

Lindsay had her hand raised, too. "Mr. Gibbons?" she asked.

"Lindsay!" he said. "One more question?"

"What do I do with Chocolate in between scenes again? Did you say something yesterday about cookies?"

"I almost forgot!" He reached into his pocket and pulled out some Liver Snaps. "Chocolate loves these. One after each scene should keep her happy."

Everyone was twittering . . . chittering . . . more nervous than ever by now.

"So go on out there and break a leg, everyone!" he shouted.

The cast and crew burst into big whoops and claps.

Madison heard Ivy whisper to Rose as they walked out of the room, "Gee, I hope fatso doesn't eat all the Liver Snaps for herself." She couldn't believe Ivy could say something so cruel after all the hard work Lindsay had done.

"Hey, Finnster!" Hart called across the room. "Wait up!"

Madison felt her stomach flip-flop.

"Hey, Finnster, have you seen my Wiz cape? Mariah told me you guys did something to it."

Madison grinned. "We sewed on silver stars."

"Whoa, that sounds cool," Hart said. He ran his fingers through his brown hair. Madison could almost smell his shampoo.

"Um, excuse me . . . Hart?" someone interrupted.

It was Poison Ivy. Madison thought she had already left the room, but here she was.

"Hey, Ivy," Hart said with a sweet smile.

Madison loved watching Hart smile, but only when it was directed at her—not her enemy.

"I just wanted to make sure I told you again about getting to the cast party," Ivy told him. She was speaking directly to Hart and ignoring Madison completely. "At my house. I can give you a ride if you don't have one. I know you said your parents had to go straight home."

"I'm grabbing a ride with Drew's parents," he said, still smiling.

Ivy flipped her red hair and touched his arm. "Okay, see you later, then."

She touched his arm.

The cast shuffled into the practice room with Mrs. Montefiore. Time was flying by. Madison was just going through the motions while visions of Ivy reaching out to Hart filled her head.

Vocal warm-ups lasted ten minutes, and then Egg led the group in a round of tongue twisters. Mr. Gibbons said those made you limber all over and think fast on your feet. Aimee, Rose, and some other dancers were off in a corner, stretching their arms and legs, too.

"Señor Hart?" Mrs. Perez was standing across the room, holding his purple cape. "Come put on your costume."

It was time for *everyone* to get into the auditorium and get on their costumes. Madison realized she'd better head backstage to help the singers get into their Tin Man, Lion, and other suits—fast. The Munchkins had to be covered in green face and hand makeup, too.

On her way backstage, Madison heard one of the techies say something about there being a lot of people in the audience.

Madison went to look for Aimee and found her applying lipstick in a back room. Aimee was so happy to see her, she couldn't stop talking to take a breath.

"I just called my house to tell everyone I saved seats down near the front for them and my mother told me that your mom is riding with them—can you believe that?" Aimee blabbed.

"Really?" Madison was glad to know her mom would sit with the Gillespies instead of Dad. That took some of her worrying away.

"How are you doing, Maddie? You look funny."

"Hey, I'm not the one dressed up like a witch," Madison said.

"Is your dad bringing his new girlfriend tonight?" Aimee asked.

Madison shook her head. She didn't think Stephanie would be there. But like Gramma Helen said, "Never say never." *Oh boy.* It would be hard enough handling Mom versus Dad without another person there.

Aimee looked over at the clock. "Fifteen minutes!" she shrieked, and ran into the bathroom to pee.

Show time!

The play really had turned out to be "the thing."

It was the thing that turned Ivy, Aimee, and Fiona into witches, made Madison into a manager, and would now reunite Madison's parents.

Madison wondered how she could be the glue that held the play together and yet feel so unglued herself. She had spent a better part of the last three weeks e-mailing Bigwheels back and forth about what to do if the Big D was looming at her home. But Madison had NO ideas about what to say or do. Not really.

The idea of Mom and Dad, and even Stephanie, sitting in the audience at the exact same time made Madison want to run far, far away.

Only there was nowhere to hide. Not now.

The show must go on.

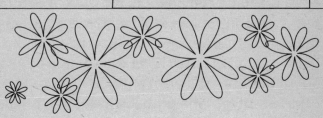

Chapter 12

When Madison walked into the auditorium just before the show, she couldn't believe her eyes. The set looked more bright and alive than ever before, with painted skyscrapers sparkling along the back wall of the stage.

The room was packed with screaming junior high school students. Madison had never seen the auditorium like this. She felt a magnetic pull from all of the energy in the room.

At her feet were piles of programs, stacked up for distribution when people were seated. Mrs. Wing had pulled together all the individual flyers from *The Wiz* and the other class shows and made one fat, twenty-page program. They were using it for all three nights of performances.

Madison was thrilled to see her own collage

copied on a page inside. She compared it to the pages from the other classes. An eighth grader had drawn a sketch for the *Guys and Dolls* section, and the director copied a New York City postcard for the ninth grade.

There had been no room for student biographies, but everyone's name was neatly listed, along with the names of everyone that had painted the set or helped with lights. Ivy had raised a little bit of a stink about this since she wanted to be as much of a show-off as possible. "She probably wanted a full page all to her own," Madison mused, "with a full-color pho-tograph and the caption 'Look at me, I'm so great!'" But the program only had her listed once.

Madison, on the other hand, found her name listed *more* than once at the bottom of the crew page.

Stage Manager and Props	*Madison Finn*
Costumes and Makeup	*Mariah Diaz, Madison Finn*
THE WIZ *Program Design*	*Madison Finn*

In a short section in the back, Mrs. Wing had also included a long list of thank-you messages from the school administration and parents. Each family had to pay ten dollars to have their greeting printed, and the money defrayed the costs of refreshments and other set expenses. It was fun to flip through and see what people had to say.

- ♥ *Congratulations to all members of the cast, especially Fiona and Chet. We're so proud of you. Mom and Dad*
- ♥ *Way to go, cast and crew of THE WIZ—you've got the chemistry for success! From 7th, 8th, and 9th grade science dept.*
- ♥ *Mr. Gibbons and the entire cast—you rock! Break a leg! Mr. and Mrs. Montefiore*
- ♥ *Felicitaciones y buena suerte en el futuro, Walter and Mariah. Con amor, Mom, Dad, and Nannie Conchita*
- ♥ *Best wishes to the seventh-grade STARS from Mrs. Goode. How can I thank you all?*

Aimee's family had paid to have the entire back cover of the program so it could be a congratulatory message *plus* an advertisement for her dad's cyber-café and book store. Aimee was tickled when she saw the message, *To Our Dancing Queen, Love, Mommy, Daddy, Roger, Billy, Dean, Doug, and Blossom.* Madison read through all the thank-you messages and saw one for Ivy, Rose, and even Dan the Lion—but didn't find her own name anywhere.

Mr. Gibbons was directing kids on where to stand, sit, and hang out. Madison couldn't find Mrs. Perez or Mariah anywhere, but Lindsay was nearby.

"Isn't this awesome?" Lindsay asked. She had on her full costume.

"Yeah, it is," Madison said, still a bit distracted.

"I can't believe how many people are out in the lobby already," Lindsay said. "I went out to see."

Madison thought about Mom and Dad again. "How many people are out there?"

"They sold like three hundred tickets, Mrs. Montefiore told me. Imagine if they had seventh, eighth, and ninth grade performing on *one* night?" Lindsay said.

"Have you seen Mariah Diaz anywhere?" Madison asked.

"Mariah?" Lindsay asked. "You mean the one with the red streaks in her hair? She's back doing Munchkin makeup, I think."

Backstage was a full-blown disaster. At first, Madison didn't see anyone she recognized, which was a little intimidating. The backstage area was a crush of teachers, techies, and other kids in all kinds of weird makeup.

Ivy and her drones appeared suddenly out of one girls' bathroom. Ivy was all decked out in her Glinda garb, wand in hand.

"Madison!" she yelped. "Where are we supposed to go?"

Madison wanted to say, "Ivy, why don't you just go HOME." But she didn't. She pointed to a side area of the stage where she now saw half the cast gathering. Fiona waved.

"You need to go over there," she said to Ivy as she waved back. "Over by Fiona and the rest. And break a leg."

"Thanks . . . I guess," Ivy said.

Madison laughed to herself. She knew the superstition was to say, "Break a leg" for *good* luck, but that wasn't what she *really* meant. Madison was standing there focusing all her energies on the possibility that maybe Ivy actually would break one of her legs. It wasn't a nice thought. Then again, she hadn't had too many *nice* Ivy thoughts lately. She looked down at her hands and noticed how she'd chewed off all her nails this week.

Mr. Gibbons appeared, clapping for everyone's attention.

In a few minutes, the curtain would be going up.

Madison could hear the Montefiores playing the introductory music for the evening. She peeked out between the curtains and saw a sea of parents flowing down the aisle into the assembly seats. It was definitely a full house tonight. Madison still couldn't spot Mom or Dad, though. She'd have to wait and face them after *The Wiz* was over.

Principal Bernard led off the evening with a short speech about Mrs. Goode's commitment to Far Hills Junior High. He cracked a few jokes that got big laughs from the parents in the audience.

Madison held her breath. *The Wiz* was here. This was real.

"Pssst! Finnster!" Hart whispered, coming up behind Madison. "Whaddya think?" He had on the purple cape with silver stars.

"Wow," Madison gasped. "You look so . . . cool."

"You think?" he said nervously. "Thanks, Finnster. Cool." He leaned over and touched her arm when he said that.

He touched her arm.

Madison could feel the pink in her cheeks. She felt anything but cool right now. "You're welcome," she quivered as he walked away.

Her heart was pounding—hard.

"AND NOW, PRESENTING CLASS SEVEN AND SELECTIONS FROM *THE WIZ.*"

Lindsay clung to Chocolate as she walked onstage in her Dorothy costume, followed by Rose Thorn as Auntie Em and Suresh as Uncle Henry. When the lights went up, Lindsay started to sing without hesitation. Her song was originally supposed to be Auntie Em singing alone, but Mrs. Montefiore made it a duet, just like she'd done with some other songs. It was as angelic as ever.

Madison darted over to help Mariah, the Munchkins, and Aimee get onstage for the next number. Lindsay's great singing gave her a jolt of energy.

Aimee spun onstage in the "Tornado Ballet."

She wasn't onstage alone for too long, but it was close enough to a dance solo to make her happy. She was wearing a purple leotard with yellow lightning bolts sewn on the side.

Every song and dance number seemed to go more smoothly than expected. The seventh grade was getting laughs and applause in all the right places. A superstitious Madison couldn't help but think that the "bad rehearsal" theory really was true in their case. The cast and crew dress rehearsals had been minor disasters, but this real show was a smash.

"Mariah." Madison found Egg's sister standing backstage in between a Dorothy-and-Scarecrow song number. "Do I need to do anything else right now?"

Mariah just smiled. "We did it. We're four songs away from the end." She leaned over and squeezed Madison's hand.

Madison watched the rest of the numbers standing in the wings, in that space between backstage and onstage. She felt like she was hovering on the edge of a cliff, the air electric with movement and sound. Madison stood in the folds of a black curtain, holding her marked-up cue script and watching the action. Occasionally she wandered backstage where people needed help with costumes or makeup touch-ups and visited the prop closet to make sure everything was still in order for the final scene. But mostly Madison stayed right there in that in between space until the end of the show.

She was in the middle of *everything* there, and she liked it.

"Ease on Down the Road" was one of the best numbers. Dan the Lion took a header during his dance part, but it was so funny, people thought it was a planned part of the show. Egg didn't have the best singing voice, but he was also getting a lot of laughs. Tommy Kwong, as usual, was a hit. His floppy Scarecrow got rip-roaring cheers.

Fiona's song as the evil Evillene got a roar of applause, too. She looked fantastic in her gray makeup and black hat. Mariah had helped her to affix a fake nose, too, with a giant, bulbous wart on the tip. Casting the nice girl as the bad witch had been a fun choice by Mr. Gibbons, and Fiona was surprisingly good at hamming up the obnoxious parts. Madison didn't ever want to see Fiona being anything but spaced out and sweet in real life, however. There were enough witches at Far Hills already.

Glinda and Addaperle's duet was a success. When Ivy and Aimee rushed offstage, Aimee danced right over to give Madison a big, sweaty hug.

"How was I?" Aimee asked. She was bouncing all over the place.

"You're all wet," Madison said.

"I know, I'm sweating. Can you see it?" Aimee raised her arms for Madison to check.

"Nope," Madison said. She wanted to tell Aimee that her performance had been so amazing—and she wanted to tell her how much she loved it. But right now, everything else was on hold for the last musical number. They would talk more later.

Lindsay Frost was up next.

As Lindsay belted out her solo, the last song in

the show, "Home," Madison listened for the response inside the auditorium.

It suddenly got quieter than quiet.

In a place jammed with chatty junior high schoolers, parents, toddlers, and faculty, *that* said everything. For a brief moment, Lindsay wasn't labeled a "geek." She wasn't in Poison Ivy's shadow. All eyes were on her—front and center.

Lindsay Frost was the most popular.

Just before the last song started, as Mrs. Montefiore clinked her opening chord, Madison saw a slow haze drift across the stage. It lifted up all the music—and then Lindsay's voice—up and out into the auditorium. Madison could actually see dust lingering in the light beams like magic powder.

The show had cast a powerful spell on the seventh grade, and it would stay with Madison and everyone even after the curtain fell. Madison watched the entire cast and crew rush the stage for bows, leaping into the air and screaming with the excitement that comes when the show is finally over.

"Wooo-hoooo!" Egg yelled out. He and Hart were high fiving all over the place.

As the curtain bobbed back up, the seventh graders finished taking their group bows, and Ivy and Aimee presented Mr. Gibbons with flowers. Madison was right there, in the corner of the stage, watching them. But this time, she didn't mind seeing her enemy and friend doing something together.

That was their job—and she knew hers.

She knew where she fit in. She really had been the glue.

Fiona and Aimee grabbed Madison to go out toward the lobby as the crowd dispersed. Families were waiting to greet everyone there.

"I can't wait to see my parents!" Fiona squealed.

"All of my brothers came—could you die?" Aimee said.

Madison gulped. It was the Mom-and-Dad moment of truth.

She rushed off with her friends to the front of the building and searched the crowd. She searched for Mom on one side, and Dad on the other. What would she say to them? What if Stephanie *was* here?

"I'll never find them!" she said. The lobby was packed.

Then, over by the table with the soda and brownies, Madison saw Mom's cobalt blue coat.

She was talking to Dad.

Chapter 13

"Slow down, honey bear!" Mom gasped as Madison zipped over.

Madison almost crashed into the table with little cups of water on trays.

"Whoa, Maddie," Dad said, opening his arms to shield her from the table's edge. He gave her a big hug. "Guess you're a little excited?"

"Yeah, well . . ." Madison didn't know what to say. "How long have you guys been talking?"

Mom and Dad turned to each other and smiled.

"Your father got here on time for the start of the show, Maddie. Can you believe it?" Mom said.

Dad shifted from foot to foot. "I'm not sure I believe it, Frannie," he said to Mom. "Must be your influence."

"I really enjoyed the performance," Mom said, changing the subject. "Especially Aimee and Fiona and . . . who's that other girl? Your old friend Ivy. They make great witches."

Madison couldn't believe Mom liked the witch part best.

"I liked the props," Dad said. "And the set and the costumes and . . . let's see, what else did *you* do, Maddie? I liked that best."

"Aw, Dad," Madison said.

"Did you see our note to you in the program?" Mom asked.

Madison made a face. "Note?"

Dad opened the program. "Yeah, I think it's somewhere here in the middle." He pointed.

♥ *Madison, we love watching you "ease on down the road"*
   to success in everything you do! Great job!
   Mom, Dad & Phinnie

Madison stared at the page and then at her parents.

"Thanks . . ." she whispered.

They hadn't forgotten.

Hart was standing only a few feet away. Madison saw him talking to two women, one who looked like she might be his grandmother.

"Hey, Finnster!" Hart said when he saw Madison looking.

"Hey, Hart."

"This is my *ya ya*," he said, introducing the older woman. He seemed sorta embarrassed. "Uh . . . that means 'grandmother' in Greek," he added.

The old woman had a sweet face with soft wrinkles all over.

"Ya Ya," Hart said. "This is Madison. Remember I told you, she's the one who made the cape."

"Ahhh, yes." The old woman took Madison's hand in hers and squeezed. Her hand was covered in smooth lines, too. "Hart tells me you did the costumes. You must be so very proud."

Hart's mother was there, too. "Madison Finn? Is that you? I haven't seen you since before we moved!" She reminded Madison about a time when she slugged Hart in the playground back in first grade. "Things have changed a lot since then, right?" Mrs. Jones laughed. "It's so nice to see you two together again. Are your mom and dad here?"

Hart and Madison both looked down at the floor. Parents could be so clueless. She reintroduced Mrs. Jones and Ya Ya to her mom and dad.

"Nice to meet you, Hart," Mom said. When no one was looking, Mom leaned over and whispered to Madison, "He's cute, Maddie."

Madison blanched white. "Mom!" she gasped softly, praying that Hart hadn't heard.

Mom winked and leaned in. "I know, I know. I won't say any more."

Dad and Ya Ya were talking about Greece the whole time. He'd lived over there for a year when he was a kid.

Meanwhile Hart disappeared to the other side of the room with Chet and Egg. They were talking to Rose and Joanie.

Madison wanted to gag.

She watched the hordes of people swirling around the room: mothers and fathers and sisters and brothers and students from all the grades in Far Hills Junior High. Everyone was buzzing in a figure eight from the brownie table to the auditorium doors to the parking lot.

Except Madison's parents.

Her mom and dad stood in the same place—next to each other the entire time. If she didn't know any better, Madison would have thought that her parents were still together. They were standing there like they always did for her whole life, laughing and nodding like nothing would ever come between them.

"Maddie!" Fiona shrieked from a few feet away. She hurried over. "Can you believe it's over? I am so bummed."

"Yeah," Madison said, glancing at Mom and Dad again. Endings *were* sad.

Aimee came over right after that, trailed by Mr. and Mrs. Gillespie and the entire Gillespie brotherhood. Roger, Billy, and Dean congratulated Madison and chatted up her parents. Doug, the Gillespie ninth grader, qickly disappeared, looking for a few of his friends.

"Do you want a ride to the cast party?" Aimee asked, hugging Madison's shoulder.

Madison pulled away. "The cast party?"

"Yeah!" Aimee said. "Oh my God, it should be great. Everyone is going."

Madison couldn't believe it. In the chaos of the crowd and Mom and Dad's reunion, she had forgotten something so important.

The cast party.

At Poison Ivy's house.

"*Everyone* is going to be there." Fiona giggled. She was looking around the room. "Including Egg. He's going, right?"

"Fiona!" Aimee said. She still cringed whenever Fiona brought up his name, which she did at every opportunity.

"Ivy didn't exactly invite me," Madison said. "I don't know if I—"

"You're invited, Maddie! *Everyone* is gonna be there," Aimee said.

"But Ivy and I—" Madison started to say.

"Forget Ivy," Aimee declared. "The cast party is the absolute best part of the show, Madison. It's the whole point. If you don't go, I won't go."

"It's just that—"

"Maddie, it's a cast party, not *her* party! She may be a good witch in the play—"

Fiona interrupted. "But she's a bad witch in real life."

They all laughed.

When Madison slipped backstage again to get her orange bag, she bumped into Lindsay. Lindsay was sitting at one of the mirrors in the dressing room, brushing out her hair.

"Oh," Lindsay said, surprised to see Madison in the mirror's reflection. "I was just getting ready to go home."

"Home? What about the cast party? You have to go to the cast party. Everyone's going to be there," Madison said.

"Nah, I don't think so." Lindsay sighed.

"But you're Dorothy! You're the star of the show!"

Lindsay smiled. "Yeah, of the show, maybe, but not the party. I don't feel like it. In case you didn't notice, I don't exactly have a million friends."

Madison sat in the chair next to Lindsay. "What do you mean? You have friends."

Lindsay ran the brush through her hair again. "Forget it."

"You have friends, Lindsay. I'm your friend."

Lindsay turned to Madison. "That's nice of you, Madison. But I know we were just friends during the show. It's okay."

It was definitely NOT okay.

Madison thought about Aimee and Ivy pretending to get along during *The Wiz*. Was she doing the same thing with Lindsay?

"Lindsay, you have to come to the cast party. Come with us."

"Us?"

"Me and Aimee and Fiona."

"That's okay. *Really.* You go."

Madison stood up again. "You sure?"

Lindsay nodded. She pulled her hair back on both sides with her heart barrettes.

"You should really wear your hair down," Madison said. "It looks better that way."

Lindsay looked into the mirror. "Really?" She took the clips out.

"And you should really go to the party, too," Madison added.

Lindsay stood up and started to pack her bag. She shook her head. "Maybe another time. I'm just not into it. Not tonight."

"How are you getting home?" Madison asked.

"I'll just walk."

"By yourself?" Madison cried.

Lindsay laughed softly. "I always do."

"Where are your parents?" Madison asked.

"They don't come to these things," Lindsay said simply. "But it's okay."

It was definitely NOT okay.

Lindsay started to walk away from the dressing tables. "See you later, Madison. Thanks again for everything."

Madison waved her arms up. "Hey, wait! I still

really think you should come to the party. Won't you just come for a little while?"

"Maybe." Lindsay waved and disappeared into the bathroom.

Madison got her own bag and went off to find Aimee, Fiona, and her ride to the cast party. She was disappointed that nothing she'd said seemed to help with Lindsay.

Aimee was standing out in front of the school building, spinning around. Her brother Roger was pulling the van up. Fiona stood nearby, chatting with Mr. Gibbons. He had Chocolate on a leash.

"Fantastic," the teacher said, clapping Madison on the back. "What fine work, Madison. Just grand."

Roger pulled up, and they all got into the van.

"Good-bye, Mr. Gibbons," Aimee yelled out. "See you at the party!"

Madison sank into the backseat and stared out the window as they pulled away. *The Wiz* was over. She felt relief and sadness at the same time.

"Lindsay didn't want to come?" Fiona asked.

Aimee nodded. "Yeah, where is she?"

Madison shrugged. "She went home."

"Hey." Aimee nudged her brother. "What reeks?"

Roger's van smelled funny, like old socks. Fiona and Madison pinched their noses and Aimee fanned hers.

"I don't smell anything," Roger said. He opened

144

the window and a rush of cool, fall wind blew in.

"That's better, stinky," Aimee said. Fiona and Madison were laughing in the backseat.

"You guys were dynamite onstage tonight," Roger said, peering into his rearview mirror to see Madison and Fiona in the backseat. "And offstage, too, Miss Stage Manager."

Madison felt herself blush a little. Just like Dad, Roger knew how to say the right things. If she had to have a runner-up crush on anyone in the whole world, it would be Roger Gillespie, with his stinky car and all.

When they arrived at the Daly house, Roger could barely get into the driveway. There were too many cars dropping off kids and parking at the side of the road. Everyone really *was* there.

When the three friends walked into Ivy's front hallway, it was like walking into a magazine spread from *House Beautiful.* Mrs. Daly had little china dishes set out on each table with peanuts and other snacks. The dining room table was decorated with flowers and punch bowls. Everywhere she looked, Madison saw food, people, and more food. Mrs. Daly was floating from room to room, making sure the guests were eating. She had on a witch hat like the ones from *The Wiz.*

"Hey, Madison!" Drew came over and said hello to the three girls. "There are these little pizzas inside, and everyone is hanging out in the den."

Aimee answered for everyone. "Thanks for the info, Drew."

Chet bounced over with Hart in tow.

Hart.

"Hey, Finnster!" he said. "Hey, Aim and Fiona."

Madison couldn't take her eyes off him. He wasn't wearing his glasses, and he looked cuter than cute. As he walked toward the food, Madison started to follow, but then she heard a familiar voice. A voice she didn't expect to hear.

Lindsay?

She turned to see Lindsay hanging up her coat in the front hall closet with Mr. Daly's assistance. Her hair was down like it had been in the dressing room.

"Hey, look who's here!" Aimee saw her, too.

"She looks different," Fiona said. "What's different?"

Madison smiled. *Everything* was different. Lindsay had taken Madison's advice and turned up for the party.

As Madison rushed over, she noticed people staring at Lindsay. Wearing her hair down had made all the difference.

Lindsay looks *pretty*, Madison thought.

The house was filling up quicker than quick. Kids crammed into the different rooms, while a fleet of teachers made their way to the hors d'oeuvres table. Madison overheard Mr. Gibbons asking Mrs. Wing what she thought of cheese puffs and spinach dip.

146

Mr. and Mrs. Montefiore had already taken a seat at the Daly piano and were playing a jazzy tune.

Aimee came over to Madison and Lindsay. "Let's go scope out the action in the other room," she said.

"Okeydokey," Lindsay replied. She tugged on her black cowl-neck sweater.

They both followed Aimee out the door.

"Maybe the party won't be so awful after all," Madison said to Aimee, smiling.

Chapter 14

Chet was showing everyone at the party how he could balance a spoon on the end of his nose. Aimee tried, too, but kept dropping it.

Drew and Egg were busy throwing peanuts into their mouths. Egg flicked one over toward Hart.

"No way, man—I'm allergic to peanuts!" Hart said.

Madison made a mental note. She'd have to add that information into her Hart file—NO PEANUTS.

"Come on, you guys," Madison said. She wanted some punch.

"Did you hear about Mrs. Wing?" Fiona said.

"What?" Madison said. She couldn't believe she didn't know something about her favorite teacher.

"I heard that her husband is a spy," Fiona said.

"Get OUT!" Aimee laughed.

"Seriously," Fiona continued. "Or a detective. Anyway, he's supposedly really cute."

Madison knew Mrs. Wing's husband would be cute.

"Didn't they just get married or something?" Aimee asked.

Madison's head spun. There were so many things she knew nothing about.

They all walked over to the drink table. Mrs. Daly had food and beverage stations set up all over her house.

Madison looked for Lindsay as Aimee poured her a drink. Lindsay was right there on a sofa, talking to a techie and another teacher, Mr. Lynch. He was the faculty advisor who helped set up the show's light board.

"Excuse me." Poison Ivy pushed Madison to the left to get a cup of pineapple punch. "Having a good time?" she asked, smirking.

Madison shrugged. "Sure," she said.

"Really?" Ivy said, sipping her punch.

"Um . . . where's the bathroom?"

"We have three," Ivy shot back. "You can use the one down there next to the den."

As Madison wandered out of the bathroom, she made her way into the Dalys' den. She was attracted to all the books. Shelves had been lined with leather volumes, and an antique spoon collection hung framed on one wall. Silver frames gleamed like

149

they'd been polished this morning.

Everything felt a little untouchable, kind of like Poison Ivy herself.

Madison saw a photograph of Ivy that must have been taken back when they were in second grade. The photo seemed so familiar, and it took Madison a moment to realize why.

She'd been there.

In the picture, Ivy was seated on a log and her head was thrown back, midlaugh. Madison remembered that *she* was the one who made Ivy crack up that day. She had been standing just outside the frame of the photograph when it had been taken. Back then, Ivy and Madison knew how to make each other crack up on command.

Madison remembered everything about that day, from cherry ice cream cones to sitting on the log in the photo, making frog noises.

"Hey!" Aimee burst into the den, talking a mile a minute. "Oh my God, Maddie, what are you doing in here? You have to come into the living room and see what Hart Jones is doing. He knows these magic tricks and it is way cool. Come on!"

Madison followed Aimee back into the bustle of the party. A bunch of kids and teachers had gathered around the coffee table. Hart was kneeling down.

"Okay, Egg, pick a card," he was saying. "Any card."

Egg cracked, "What is that, a fixed deck or something?"

"Just pick a card, man," Chet said.

Egg pulled a card out of the deck and looked at it. He put it back again. After shuffling the deck, Hart went through each card until he reached the jack of diamonds. He looked up at Egg.

"No WAY! How did you know that?" Egg said.

Everyone laughed.

Madison watched as Hart did the trick again for Egg's sister, Mariah. Once again, he identified the right card.

"He's like a real wizard," Fiona said. Hart had put on his purple cape with the stars again as a joke.

Madison wished she had the nerve to go over and do the trick with Hart, but she didn't. She just watched as he flashed the cards to the rest of the group.

"Hey, Madison." Lindsay came up to her, smiling.

"Hey." Madison grinned. "I'm glad you came to the party, Lindsay."

"I was leaving the building and Mr. Gibbons saw me walking away. He said he wouldn't let me go home alone, so he gave me a ride over. He's so nice."

Madison nodded. "It's a fun party. Are you glad you're here?"

"I'm really here because of you," Lindsay said softly. "You were right about everything. So thanks for that. Thanks for being a real friend."

Madison couldn't help but smile.

Ivy was perched on a chair across the room. She announced, "Sundaes in the kitchen! Does anyone want ice cream?"

Everyone hustled in. No one would turn down homemade sundaes. Mrs. Daly had hot fudge and whipped cream and a whole lineup of toppings, on the counter. Ivy was waving an ice-cream scoop around like it was a magic wand.

As fate would have it, Madison ended up in the ice cream line next to Hart.

Magic.

"Cool tricks you were doing in there," she said.

"Thanks, Finnster," he said. "My dad got me magic lessons for my birthday last year. I know a pretty cool rope trick, too. I'll show you sometime."

"Hello, Hart." Ivy appeared with a bowl of ice cream. She handed it to him. "If you want toppings, they're all over there."

He grabbed the bowl and walked away. "See ya, Finnster."

Ivy looked at Madison and tilted her head to one side. "Having fun yet?" she said. "Everyone says my party is great."

Madison didn't want to be rude. "Everything's great, Ivy."

Ivy shrugged. "I know." She walked away.

Aimee was standing away from the ice cream and sauces. Madison went over to talk to her.

"No ice cream, Aim?" she asked.

Aimee shook her head. "Nope. I have to watch what I eat. I don't want to get all bloated."

Aimee was always worrying about her body. She said she needed to be careful because of dance. She wanted to look good in her leotard. Madison thought she looked just fine.

Fiona wasn't worried about anything, however. She had piled ice cream, caramel sauce, and nuts in a bowl and was headed across the room toward Egg. She'd probably be back for seconds, too.

"Look at that," Madison said to Aimee when she saw where Fiona was headed. "Look who Fiona is sitting with."

"Oh my God!" Aimee said. "What do you think they're talking about?"

"I dunno."

Now it was Aimee and Madison's turn to giggle.

"Pssst! Look at that guy over *there*," Aimee said. She nodded in the direction of a tall kid with a crew cut. He looked like he had an earring. He'd been one of the techies who'd helped to rig Emerald City and some of the other set pieces, including the oversized trees Mom helped get.

"He's in ninth grade, isn't he?" Madison asked.

Aimee raised her eyebrows. "So?"

Madison pushed her friend. "Aimee, I can't believe you."

"I'm gonna go talk to him," she said.

Madison watched as Aimee approached the nameless ninth grader. She didn't stop smiling once. Aimee sure knew how to get a guy's attention. Madison wondered what magic was involved in that.

The party kept up until almost nine-thirty. Madison didn't see Lindsay again, so she figured she must have left.

Fiona was hanging out with Chet, Egg, and Drew on a sofa, talking about computer games. Fiona was sitting right next to Egg. Madison wondered if they *would* start dating. She pushed that out of her thoughts real quick.

"Guess what?" Aimee suddenly reappeared with a giant smile. She said that her brother Roger would be coming to pick them up in a few minutes.

"What happened to that ninth grader?"

"He was nice," Aimee said, not revealing much detail.

"So what are you gonna do?" Madison asked.

Aimee shrugged. She had no idea what she would do. It was just fun to flirt.

"You know what?" Aimee asked all of a sudden. "You're a great friend!"

Madison was surprised. "Why are you saying that, Aimee?"

"Because. You're so nice. To me. To Lindsay. . . ." Aimee's voice trailed off. "Seventh grade just stresses me out and I'm not so good at being nice. I know that."

"You're great, too," Madison said, wrapping her

arm around Aimee's shoulder. "You're my best, best friend."

Aimee had a big grin on her face. "We made it to junior high, Maddie. We used to talk about this. Parties. Boys. All of it. And now . . ."

Madison sighed. "We're really here."

With arms locked, they glanced around the room. Madison had come this far and now she wished she could just go a little more. If only she could flirt better! Madison hadn't spoken more than five words to Hart since the party started. And even when she did speak, Ivy always showed up in the middle of it.

Drew came strolling over to Madison. "I just wanted to say good-bye," he said. "So, good-bye." Just like that, he walked away, before Madison had a chance to say anything. He and Egg and a bunch of other guys left, too.

Where was Hart?

Madison, Fiona, and Aimee grabbed their coats and bags and walked toward the front door. Just when she thought she'd missed seeing her crush, Madison spotted him. He was standing in the living room—and she saw him but knew he hadn't seen her yet because he didn't yell, "Finnster!"

There was another reason he didn't say anything. Ivy Daly.

She was hunched over, leaning on a desk right next to him. She was scribbling something on a pad of paper.

Was Ivy giving Hart her number?

Madison turned right around and ran straight through the front door, scuttling out of the Daly house so fast that Aimee and Fiona could barely catch her.

Once they were inside Roger's van, Madison didn't say one word about what she'd seen, even though Aimee and Fiona suspected that something had suddenly gone very wrong.

Madison wouldn't tell. It was a *secret* secret—next to the files, next to Bigwheels.

How could Ivy have given Hart her number?

Madison asked herself that question at least ten times. She wondered why she liked the real-life Wizard so much that it made her sides ache. She couldn't list reasons. It wasn't about lists. She just FELT it.

That's what *The Wiz* was all about, anyway, wasn't it? You had to hold on to your dreams. Especially the dreamy ones like Hart.

Madison gave Mom an enormous hug when she walked in the door at home. Mom and Phin had been up watching TV and waiting for Madison's return. Phinnie waddled over, half asleep, too. He yawned.

"Well?" Mom asked curiously. "Talk! How was the party? How's that cute boy?" She wanted the whole scoop—and nothing but the scoop.

Madison filled Mom in on the food stations, the magic tricks, and the rest. Then she yawned, just like

Phinnie had. No talk about cute boys tonight, Madison explained.

"I have to go to bed, Mom."

Phin followed Madison up to her messy room. He made himself comfortable on her bed pillows as she opened her laptop. Madison hoped that maybe this was one of those late nights when Bigwheels would be online when she wasn't supposed to be. She logged on to bigfishbowl.com.

It was a busy Friday under the sea.

And Bigwheels *was* online.

```
<MadFinn>: You're here!!!!
<Bigwheels>: what a surprise how
    cool
<MadFinn>: (((Bigwheels)))
<Bigwheels>: thx whassup?
<MadFinn>: FIRST how r ur parents
<Bigwheels>: :-Z LOL
<MadFinn>: No! I mean with splitting
    up
<Bigwheels>: kewl
<MadFinn>: still together?
<Bigwheels>: sort of
<Bigwheels>: I'm not so worried
<MadFinn>: @—)—(—
<Bigwheels>: is that a flower???
<MadFinn>: yup
<Bigwheels>: thanks for advice it
    helped sooo much
```

\<MadFinn\>: really?

\<Bigwheels\>: totally

\<MadFinn\>: I had our cast party tonite

\<Bigwheels\>: and? What happened with your crush?

\<MadFinn\>: CUL8R

\<Bigwheels\>: what?

\<MadFinn\>: he's seeing someone else I think

\<Bigwheels\>: bummer

\<MadFinn\>: me and boys are 100% hopeless I swear!

\<Bigwheels\>: that is SO not true

\<MadFinn\>: what about u?

\<Bigwheels\>: hopeless LOL

\<MadFinn\>: how is school 4 you?

\<Bigwheels\>: I have a HUGE english essay due and I'm writing on The Lost Princess of Oz. You inspired me.

\<MadFinn\>: I did?

\<Bigwheels\>: GTG

\<MadFinn\>: are your parents watching?

\<Bigwheels\>: Mom just found me on the computer

\<MadFinn\>: whoops

\<Bigwheels\>: guess they weren't sleeping

\<MadFinn\>: bye

<Bigwheels>: WB
<Bigwheels>: *poof*

Before she closed down her computer, Madison had to get into her files. So much had happened tonight, and she couldn't risk forgetting any of it.

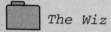 *The Wiz*

So it's over. The sky didn't fall in on my head, the stage didn't collapse, and no lives were lost during the making of this show. I would say the only thing that *was* lost during *The Wiz* was my nervousness.

Rude Awakening: Just when you feel like you're on a yellow brick road to nowhere . . . something great happens.

I'm not quite sure what I expected from Oz. Sometimes I do things because everyone else is, or I like people (or DON'T like people) because everyone else does. I want to be liked, too. But meeting Lindsay changed my feelings. I don't even know if I will stay friends with Lindsay after this, but I will try.

I think that I am a combo of every character in the play right now. I've gotten smarter, I felt more stuff in my heart, and I also got braver. I hate to admit that parents are right, but they are—sometimes. Dad would be glad to know that I learned all these things from doing the play. His pep talks worked lots. So did Mom's.

The characters in *The Wiz* couldn't get through Oz without friends and the same is totally true for me. My list includes old friends like Aimee, new friends like Fiona, and even friends that I didn't expect like Lindsay Frost. And online friends. I can't forget Bigwheels!

Madison signed off and shut down her computer. If she didn't get some sleep soon, she'd be destroyed tomorrow. She wanted to be in good spirits for dinner with Dad and Stephanie and for hanging out with her friends. Plus, she had so much homework to catch up on. Luckily, Mr. Danehy had agreed to move the big science test a week later.

Phin was just as pooped as Madison. He jumped up into bed with her.

"I can't go through Oz without my friends," Madison cooed into her pug's ear. "Not even my animal friends, right, Phinnie?"

He snuzzled close, looked up at her with his wet brown eyes, and snorted.

It was a doggie "yes."

Madison closed her own eyes.

Dorothy was right when she said there was no place like home. There was no place like Madison's house right now.

Especially under the covers—the safest place in the whole world.

Mad Chat Words:

%-(	Sad and confused
:-c	Bummed out
:-Z	Sleeping
QT	Cutie
CUL8R	See you later
A/S/L	Age/sex/location
ASAP	As soon as possible
IDGI	I don't get it
<rrr>	Anger
PAW	Parents are watching!
(((Bigwheels)))	Cyberhug to . . .
Kewl	Cool
@--)--(--	Rose (flower)

<u>Madison's Computer Tip:</u>

Sometimes when I'm on the computer, a whole hour can go by and I don't even realize it. **Time flies when you're online. Keep an eye on the clock and don't forget your friends.** I try to make special times (like during study hall or after dinner) for answering e-mail, chatting, writing in my files, surfing the Net, homework, and other stuff. I don't usually do all those things at once. I try to remember to spend *real* time with friends and not just Insta-Message time.

Visit Madison at www.madisonfinn.com

161

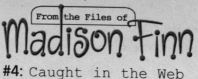

#4: Caught in the Web

Chapter 1

Madison hadn't checked her laptop computer for e-mails yet today, so she powered it up. The compuer was still sitting open on her bedroom desk exactly where she'd left it plugged in that morning. One click and the motor hummed again. After the home screen illuminated, Madison's e-mailbox flashed with a ping.

✉ Bob1A1239   Invest NOW $$$

Who was Bob1A1239? His name looked like a real name, like a person from school. It annoyed Madison to think that someone was e-mailing her while pretending to be a regular guy. He wasn't real!

She knew it must have been an advertisement and immediately deleted the message. Dad always said to do that when she didn't know the sender.

✉ Eggaway	Computer?
✉ Boop-Dee-Doop	Spooktacular SALE
✉ JeffFinn	FW: Ha Ha Halloween

Unlike Mr. Bob's message, the remaining notes in Madison's mailbox were from a more familiar crew.

Egg needed homework questions for Mrs. Wing's computer class.

Boop-Dee-Doop, a girlie online clothes store, was having a sale.

Dad had sent along another one of his jokes. Madison always tried to guess the punch line.

What do you put on a Halloween sundae?

Whipped scream was the answer. She guessed it right away, but she still giggled—hard. Dad's e-mails were like happy shots. It didn't even matter if she heard a joke before.

Madison opened a saved document and typed the sundae joke into her Dad file. It was joke number thirty-two so far this month. After that, she went into her file marked "Social Studies." She'd created folders for every single subject. Tonight she had to study terms about archaeology. Her teacher, Ms. Belden, said she might be popping a pop quiz tomorrow.

Madison didn't want to take any chances.

By the time she memorized the definitions, it was already six o'clock. Her stomach was grumbling. Her e-mailbox pinged again.

✉ Webmaster@bigfis   Are you CAUGHT IN THE

The new e-mail was an announcement from her favorite Web site, bigfishbowl.com. Text at the top flashed orange and white in honor of the season. The words looked like candy corns.

```
From: webmaster@bigfishbowl.com
To: Members Only
Subject: Are you CAUGHT IN THE WEB?
New Contest!
Date: Mon 16 Oct 5:57 PM
```
Are you caught in the WEB? Well, get snagged NOW!

The big fins at bigfishbowl.com want YOU to write us a mystery for Halloween. We provide the story starter and you provide the thrills! This is a special contest for bigfishbowl members ONLY.

Contest entries due Monday, October 30.

To enter the contest: Every winner

MUST begin with the story starter below. Write a story no more than 500 words. The winner will have their mystery posted on our site; and get a mystery game valued up to $25.

IT WAS A DARK AND STORMY NIGHT. THE SCHOOL BUILDING WAS CLOSED, BUT

INSIDE . . .

"DINNER!"

Madison jumped. The message disappeared from the screen. Her pulse was racing so hard all of a sudden that she mouse-clicked the wrong icon on her computer screen.

"Whoa! Mom scared me," Madison said to Phin.

"Madison!" the downstairs voice bellowed again. "Sorry I'm late! Is Phinnie up there with you?"

"YES!" Madison bellowed back.

"Rowrooooo!" Phinnie howled.

"Come downstairs!" Mom yelled again. "I got takeout, honey bear! Come and eat!"

Madison wasn't surprised about the menu. Mom had a habit of providing on-the-run dinners for the two of them. Madison usually categorized these meals as "Scary Dinners" in her computer files.

After inhaling the take-out Chinese vegetables and crunchy noodles, Madison started overthinking.

She thought about the contest.

She thought about ghosts.

She thought about what she wanted for dessert.

"Penny for your thoughts," Mom said gently, reaching into a white bag. She produced a slice of cake in a pink Styrofoam carton with frosting smudged on the side.

Had Mom eavesdropped on her mind? Madison stared, stunned. She contemplated the chocolate, double-buttercream universe sitting on the table.

Mmmmmm.

She couldn't wait to take the first bite.

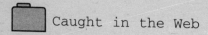 Caught in the Web

Maybe if I could write scary stories I'd win this new Caught in the Web contest on bigfishbowl. Can my writing possibly compare to Edgar Allan Poe's "The Tell-Tale Heart"?

I could write a "My Teacher Is Really a Vampire" story. I'd write it about my science teacher, Mr. Danehy, since he really bites. But who would read that?

Maybe I should just write about Ivy Daly and Hart Jones together at the school dance. Now *that's* scarier than scary.

Here's the truth: the only Halloween story I'm gonna be able to write is "The Tell-Tale Hart," without the "e" and without me.

Rude Awakening: Life gets extra tricky around Halloween.

What's Your Sign?

ASTROLOGY RULES! will give you the complete lowdown on your sign, with your own personal profile!

Find out your planetary rules. What are your planetary colors, power stones, and strong cosmic vibes? Get advice on fun, fashion, beauty, love matches, cosmic advantages, health, and learn who you truly are.

Coming soon to bookstores everywhere.

Visit us at http://www.volobooks.com

VOLO
HYPERION